*Temmi and the Flying Bears*

Other books by Stephen Elboz

The House of Rats
The Games-Board Map
Bottle Boy
The Byzantium Bazaar
Ghostlands

# Temmi and the Flying Bears

Stephen Elboz

*Illustrated by Lesley Harker*

Oxford University Press

Oxford New York Toronto

Oxford University Press, Great Clarendon Street, Oxford OX2 6DP

Oxford New York
Athens Auckland Bangkok Bogota Bombay
Buenos Aires Calcutta Cape Town Dar es Salaam Delhi
Florence Hong Kong Istanbul Karachi
Kuala Lumpur Madras Madrid Melbourne
Mexico City Nairobi Paris Singapore
Taipei Tokyo Toronto Warsaw

and associated companies in
Berlin Ibadan

*Oxford* is a trade mark of Oxford University Press

Copyright © Stephen Elboz 1998
First published 1998

The author has asserted his moral right to be
known as the author of the work.

Cover illustration by Kevin Jenkins

A CIP catalogue record for this book is available
from the British Library

ISBN 0 19 271747 2

Printed in Great Britain

In fondest memory of Gordon Blake

## *Chapter One*

Now Temmi had a fondness for all the forest bears. He knew their lairs and ways.

Cinnamon bears, he would tell you, were as agile as monkeys and climbed so quickly that they were soon lost from sight at the tops of the tallest trees; and their whines and whistles had a sadness which always made him shiver.

Sag bears couldn't be more different. Temmi often laughed aloud just to see one of these stupid creatures. They looked like something fat and overripe which had dropped to the ground. Too lazy to run away, they snoozed sitting up on their haunches, occasionally scratching themselves in their sleep and sending dust rising from their coats.

Growlers were much more secretive, prowling the densest parts of the forest. Temmi knew to admire these huge animals from a distance (or from up a tree), because growlers were so fierce that even a wolf pack would avoid crossing paths with one.

But of all the bears, Temmi's favourites by far were the flying bears.

Every day, after he finished helping his father bring in the fish from the lake, when the canoes were safely beached and the nets mended and hung up to dry, Temmi slipped away from his village and hurried into the mountains. He climbed steadily until he reached the place where the snow-fields lay all year, and icicles on rocky ledges might melt an inch or two in high summer, but never entirely disappear—just like his footprints.

On reaching a certain hill, he always stopped to scan the distant cliffs, hoping to sight his first flying bear. He was rarely disappointed.

They were gloriously white bears both in fur and feathers—although the old ones were nearer ivory, the cubs were as bright as snowflakes.

Temmi was proud that he could identify every bear in the colony, for they all had special habits or features to distinguish them; and it was Temmi

who had given each bear his name. Dorf barked like a seal; Snibpuss was inquisitive and always getting into trouble for it; Abany was vain, spending much of his time grooming himself; Ocki was greedy and rather fond of stealing other bears' fish . . .

But Temmi's favourite was Cush, the last cub born that season, born so long after the other cubs that Temmi worried that he might be too small to survive. But Pasha proved a good and loving mother to Cush. She sat on her nest of twigs keeping him warm and feeding him her milk. And he grew stronger, although naturally he was less developed than the other cubs born that year.

Apart from being a responsible parent, Pasha was a sensible one too. She knew Cush must be able to fly before the first snows came. And one day, as Temmi watched, he saw her gently nudge her cub to the edge of her nest, high up on the cliff-side. Cush yelped piteously and tried to scramble back to safety, but Pasha was firm. With one final shove, she sent her cub tumbling through the air.

Temmi gave a gasp, but he need not have worried. Instinctively, the little bear spread his downy wings and gently glided to the nearest tree, landing on a branch with an undignified scramble. Once secure he looked so pleased with himself that Temmi broke out into applause.

The little bear gazed down at him, mouth open and tongue hanging out—amused in a kind of bearlike way. And Temmi beamed back, as proud of him as Pasha was.

After that there was no stopping Cush. He turned into a real show-off, especially if Temmi was around. Then he'd practise his swoops and hovers: and when Temmi saw his fur was wet he knew he'd been learning how to catch fish from the river.

Soon Temmi was bringing him presents of fish he had stolen from his father's boat, being careful to hide them beneath his cloak. And Cush came to expect a fish from every visit, although at first he was rather puzzled, wondering why the boy should be holding up a fish in the air. Fish come from rivers, not boys, and they live in water, not air. But as Cush's wariness of Temmi faded and his confidence in flying grew, he would come diving down to gently take the fish in his paws, carrying it back to the cliff where he ate every bit, apart from the bones, the fins, and the tail (which Ocki came sniffing around for later on).

And this was how the friendship between Temmi and Cush began and developed.

## Chapter Two

The men arrived at Temmi's village one snowy winter's evening. They stood in silence, watching with grim, hard faces. They carried spears, and alongside them were wolves—hunting wolves—to which the men spoke harshly, kicking them with their boots whenever fights broke out.

As head of the village, Temmi's father stepped forward to greet them; Temmi went with him, a few paces behind, trampling his father's shadow. The rest of the village looked on in cold suspicion, unsure what to make of the men. The village dogs, however, were in no doubt. They barked frenziedly at the scent of the wolves and had to be shut away. But everyone knew the strangers must be welcomed with hospitality, that was the rule of the village.

The leader of the strangers wore coarse wolves' pelts over finer clothes. And yet Temmi scarcely noticed anything of what he wore, so fascinated was he by the man's face. Or rather his nose, for it was made of silver and was not like a human nose at all, but was snout-like, even to the extent of having two tiny tusks carved out of walrus ivory. A black silk ribbon secured the false nose in place, tied in a neat bow at the back of his head.

Finally the man spoke, his voice metallic and nasal.

'My name is Lord Thurbolt,' he said with a brisk nod and click of the heels. 'I serve Haggoth, Witch-Queen of the High Witchlands. But should you prefer, the name by which I am better known is General Tin Nose.' He smiled slyly. 'This, despite the fact that not one of my many noses is made from that particular low metal.'

'*Many noses?*' queried Temmi's father.

In answer, Tin Nose beckoned one of his men across. The fellow bowed and held out a small wooden box. Casting his cloak over one shoulder, Tin Nose flicked open the lid.

Inside, Temmi was astonished to see a number of

different metal noses set into the velvet lining. Some were animal-like, some human, and some were simply grotesque. But, as Tin Nose had boasted, none was of tin. They shone either gold or silver and many had the extra glint of a precious stone or pearl.

Tin Nose caught Temmi staring at him and lifted a hand to his face saying, 'Perhaps you would care to see the hole underneath where my real nose used to be?'

Too horrified for words, Temmi shook his head.

Tin Nose let out a great roar of laughter and, lunging at the wolves that milled about his feet, seized the largest by the throat. The wolf bristled angrily and tried to turn his head to bite, but Tin Nose held him securely and the wolf could only make threatening growls.

'This is the culprit,' he said. 'This is the villain who bit off my nose and swallowed it when he was still no bigger than a cub. Ah, Frostbite, I knew then what a fine hunting animal you'd be and I was right, although I had you severely beaten for what you did to me.'

He shook Frostbite as if strangling him, but in his rough play was affection as well as respect.

Temmi's father cleared his throat. 'You and

your men must be weary, Lord Thurbolt,' he said and he led the way to the longhouse, where the villagers held their meetings and feasts.

Once inside, Tin Nose gazed around at the wooden benches and ancient shields upon the log walls; his feet kicked at the rushes strewn over the mud floor. Without saying a word, he gave the impression he was used to better things. Then he stared contemptuously at the blazing fire at the centre of the hall, pointedly striding away from it. Behind the long tables his men whipped the wolf pack into silence.

The meal that followed soon turned into a strained affair. Tin Nose's men stared at the plates of baked fish and stewed cabbage, refusing to touch them. Some were heard to grumble, 'Have they no meat?'

Temmi and the other villagers ate in silence, glancing nervously at the wolves, who shared their masters' distaste for the food set before them, scornfully pawing the fish, or throwing it up in the air like a child with a toy.

Giving a snort of derision, Tin Nose shoved his plate aside. Temmi heard one of the villagers whisper, 'They don't care for our food or hospitality, so why are they here?'

Moments later they found out. Rising to his feet, Tin Nose addressed the company.

'I will speak briefly and plainly,' he said, as if the villagers were too stupid to understand anything else. 'We have been sent by command of the great Witch herself. She has heard of a rarity found only in these parts. A species of bear with wings. And it is her noble majesty's wish to present one of these freakish creatures to her daughter, Princess Agna.'

Hearing this, Temmi angrily jumped up. 'The flying bears aren't freaks!' he shouted. 'They are wild creatures, and you can't make a wild creature live in a cage. It will die of unhappiness!'

Tin Nose regarded him coldly, his metal nose winking in the centre of his shadowy face. 'The great Witch herself has ordered it,' he said. 'And no one shall question her orders.'

'He is very young, my lord,' apologized Temmi's father, hastily pushing Temmi back down on the bench. And he hissed, 'Hush now, boy. Do you want to incense the Witch so much that she sends the snow and frosts against us? Do you want the lake to remain frozen all summer? Is that what you want? Nothing in your belly because we can't fish.'

'But I—'

10

'Not another word, do you hear?'

Temmi nodded sullenly, but his outburst had further soured the atmosphere. Most of his neighbours secretly agreed with him but they were more afraid of the power of the Witch-Queen.

After the plates were cleared away, the villagers attempted to entertain their guests. Tin Nose openly yawned at the singing, shouting over it for his tankard to be refilled—treating the villagers as little more than servants. His men talked and laughed together as Croel played his harp.

Everyone was glad when it grew late and they had to return to their huts, leaving the strangers to bunk down in the longhouse, using the tables as beds.

Temmi went home and, too furious to speak, threw himself down on his pallet of straw. On the bed next to his, his father snored, but Temmi turned restlessly.

Outside, the bitter east wind blew across the lake. Temmi listened to it for a long time until his eyelids grew heavy and he slowly drifted into sleep.

## Chapter Three

Temmi awoke suddenly with a wolf's howl still ringing clear and terrible in the air.

It hadn't arisen from the longhouse.

Moments later a second wolf answered from the other side of the village.

A man shouted.

A woman screamed.

Snatching up his fishing knife, Temmi's father dashed out into the freezing night. Temmi followed, wrapped in his blanket, his breath frost-white in the moonlight.

'What is it?' Temmi's father shouted. 'What's happening?'

Cuddie the old fisherman came hobbling out

of the shadows. Temmi's father raised his knife higher until he recognized him and lowered it again.

'It's the Witch's men,' gasped Cuddie. 'They've upped and gone.'

'Gone?'

Cuddie nodded. 'The men have gone, but not the wolves. The wolves are all around the village driving our people back.'

Temmi's father scowled angrily. 'What on earth do they mean by this?'

But Temmi knew at once. 'They've gone after the flying bears!' he cried and, before either man could stop him, he ran off into the darkness.

'Come back, boy!' shouted his father.

But Temmi ran on, past the huts and his dismayed neighbours who stood around in helpless groups, until he reached the ditch that marked the edge of the village. He saw immediately it was as Cuddie had described. The wolves swept by in a straggling pack, some along the bottom of the ditch like shadows, those at the top wearing the gloss of the moon on their coats.

Suddenly, and before he had time to do anything, a large dark shape broke free and launched itself at him. Temmi briefly glimpsed claws and fangs and a narrowed pair of yellow eyes—then the wolf's forepaws struck him mid chest. He fell back shocked and winded. The wolf remained on top of him and Temmi saw it was Frostbite.

The animal sniffed him as if sniffing food, his wet snout thrusting into every hollow of Temmi's face. Sick with terror, Temmi remembered Tin Nose and how he had earned his nickname; and he tried picturing himself with his own metal nose. His father was too poor to afford silver. Perhaps he could make him an iron nose from an old cooking-pot.

Triumphant, and with his paws still pressing upon Temmi's body, Frostbite threw back his head and his throat rippled to a long eerie howl, as if trying to shatter the moon like glass; then he leapt off Temmi, turning in mid air, and scudded down the bank and up the other side, until he was once more leading his snarling pack around the village.

Temmi sat up, too angry to feel hurt. Then his father was there, dragging him to his feet.

'Stupid, stupid boy,' he blazed. 'What did you hope to achieve against the Witch's servants?' He ran his hand through his hair, growing more calm. 'Did they hurt you?' he asked.

Temmi shook his head. He knew his father

was right to be so angry, especially as the wolves were running hungry. But he was not a baby, he could take care of himself. And he resented the way his father gripped his arm as they hurried to the safety of the longhouse where the entire village now gathered.

Inside, the air was churned up with excitement and confusion. Everyone was speaking at once. Words tumbled out, but nobody listened to anyone else. Temmi saw that the men stood armed with fishing knives; and from the walls the shields were being carefully handed down. The dust on them made the men feel ashamed.

Climbing on to one of the long tables, Temmi's father made the hall silent by stamping down his foot hard, as if he was crushing the noise like a beetle beneath his heel. The villagers turned to stare at him.

'I know you are all angry,' he told them. 'You are right to be. The Witch's men have treated our hospitality with contempt. Now her wolves surround the village making a living wall and us her prisoners inside it. For safety's sake we must remain together here in the longhouse. Wolves can see better than us in the dark. In the morning, if they have not gone, we shall drive them back into the forest with our knives.'

Heads nodded in agreement. The fire was banked higher and the children were settled beneath the tables. By the door, men stood on guard. They looked down at their knives and wished for swords.

Outside, the wolves bayed, one answering another from every point around the village—and sometimes from inside it too.

Temmi fell asleep sitting up against the longhouse wall. He awoke shivering as the men were getting ready to go out. He overheard them discussing the wolves, some men reporting that they had gone at dawn, melting silently into the forest. He also overheard them making plans to follow, to make sure Tin Nose's company had left their lands for good.

Leaping up, Temmi tugged at his father's sleeve. 'Pa-Pa. Let me come with you. Please, Pa!'

His father looked sternly at him, on the point of refusing, but Donmar the carpenter said, 'Let the boy come. After all, he is nearly old enough to take out his own canoe on the lake.' And with a shrug his father relented.

'But don't whine or complain if you get tired or cold,' he warned. 'Now go and fetch my second-best knife for yourself, the one with the notched blade that I keep under my bed.'

Temmi ran to his hut. The village was oddly silent. The cocks, still locked away, had not crowed because they had been tricked into believing that their little coop was all night-time itself. Snatching up the old knife from its hiding-place, Temmi raced back to join the men who had already started off from the longhouse.

They gathered at the ditch gazing in silence at the endless rings of pawprints in the snow and, to satisfy themselves that the wolves had really gone, they walked all around the village. At one point they saw the tracks break away and stream off into the forest.

'They're heading for the mountains,' said one of the men.

'The flying bears!' uttered Temmi.

'The bears can look after themselves,' said his father. 'Even if Tin Nose finds them he'll never be able to catch one. The flying bears are too cunning.'

Despite his father's words, Temmi felt as if he was on the edge of something quite terrible. He knew Tin Nose would never return to the Witch empty handed.

They followed the tracks through the forest

and up the steep slopes, walking in each other's footprints where the snow lay deepest.

'Look!' cried old Cuddie, pointing up.

A flying bear wheeled high in the cloudless sky. Temmi recognized the bear as Beog, Cush's father, and he noticed how agitated he was, and how he acted with uncharacteristic wariness, tracking the men at a distance. This only added to Temmi's unease, and he kept running ahead, urging the men to follow more quickly.

At last they arrived at the clearing, with the bears' nesting colony rising sheer before them—and Temmi knew something was badly wrong. The bears sat silently on the ledges, wings folded, staring down at the intruders. From them Temmi sensed a brooding resentment he had never known before, and then he saw the reason for it. The splash of red and the hateful arrow with its black crow-feathers.

He yelled and bounded forward. If it wasn't for the blood, the bear might have been mistaken for another mound of snow, its wings half opened and crumpled beneath it.

It was Pasha.

Temmi gripped the black arrow that had taken her life. He gripped and pulled. The arrow was deeply lodged, but as his fury turned to strength it came free. He broke the shaft and casting the pieces away threw himself over Pasha's body, sobbing uncontrollably into the white fur.

The men gathered round, watching him and feeling awkward.

Suddenly Temmi remembered Cush and clawing the tears from his eyes scanned the ledges for sight of him.

'Cush! Cush!' he called. But Cush was not there, and Temmi understood at once; he understood that Pasha had been killed for the sole purpose of luring her cub to the ground. In truth, the bears' cunning had proved useless against simple brutality and Tin Nose now possessed what he had come for.

The bears glowered down at the boy who shouted at them. All at once and together they broke into an angry barking, leaning over the ledges, some beating their wings. Their thoughts were quite clear. Men were murderers and takers of the young. Men were not to be trusted.

## Chapter Four

Nobody knew how much the flying bears meant to Temmi, not even his father, who now stepped forward. Temmi felt a hand gently stroke his shoulders but shrugged it off, refusing to be consoled or even listen to his father.

Still his father tried. He offered to let Temmi carry his best knife back to the village. He promised him bread spread with honey from their precious store, which was their only source of sweetness for the entire winter. He promised to build Temmi his own canoe and give him his five best fish-hooks.

But Temmi continued to sob and rake his fingers through Pasha's fur.

After kindness failed, his father tried a firmer line. 'Come on, Temmi, end all this nonsense,' he said bluntly. 'What is one flying bear against the safety of the village? Let the Witch's men have the bear cub. Be thankful they have gone and left us in peace.'

Temmi glared up with savage red-rimmed eyes. Without the Witch's men there, all his anger flew towards his father for his unthinking words. He leapt up and began to run, scrambling wildly through the snow.

'Come back, Temmi!' shouted some of the men.

'Oh, let him go,' sighed his father wearily. 'He is best left to himself for a while.'

The men turned and made their way back down to the village. But Temmi's father was wrong about his son. He had not run away to be alone, he had gone to follow the Witch's men and rescue Cush. It was not grief that drove him but fury.

Even with tears blurring his vision, the tracks Temmi followed showed clearly in the snow. Men's boot-marks and wolves' pawprints. The first stretching away in straight purposeful lines, the second scuttering busily between interesting smells: but both headed deep into the mountains.

Temmi kept his eyes fixed on the tracks. He thought of Cush and sometimes of his father, but never once did he think to turn back.

Night came quickly upon him. The snow turned silver, then grey, and the tracks filled with darkness, like tiny pools of water. Only then did Temmi realize he had no food and was growing steadily colder. He lifted his head. In the distance he saw firelight. Tin Nose had stopped to set up camp, yet the fire was not for warmth or cooking, but to keep the snow leopards at bay.

The light lay deceptively far off, but as Temmi crept up to it, dodging from one pine tree to the next, he heard Tin Nose talking to his men. 'Get yourselves bedded down,' he ordered. 'We set off before first light and a long trek lies ahead of us.'

The men shuffled away to dig themselves burrows in the snow, roughly calling the wolves to come to them and manhandling the creatures into place before them like living doors. The wolves had been trained to obey, and laying their heads on their paws, went to sleep.

Temmi watched this safely at a distance. He was hunter enough to keep downwind of the camp so the wolves didn't sense him there. Apart from the men and wolves, Temmi also saw a roughly made cage. Inside it a small white creature restlessly turned, now and again standing absolutely still to whimper and listen for its mother.

'Oh, poor Cush,' murmured Temmi, his heart going out to the little bear. 'He hasn't enough room to stretch his wings.'

He saw two moist brown eyes peer out through the bars, and certain that the rest of the camp was now fast asleep, Temmi stole up as silently as he could, which was not easy, for snow does not muffle footsteps, it creaks and groans, and the skin of frost upon it split and cracked. At every step he fully expected one of the wolves to raise its eager head. But the pack slept on and the men's snores sounded faint from beneath the banks of snow.

At first Temmi's shadow was cast by the blue light of a million pulsating stars but, as he neared the centre of the camp, the firelight re-cast it and angled it a different way. Temmi blinked through the flames. The wolves might have been pelts spread over the snow so still did they lie.

By this time he was very close to the cage. He saw a snuffling nose poke from it, only to quickly disappear and reappear in another place—and another, until Cush was perfectly sure about who he could scent. Then his entire rump waggled,

because his tail was far too small and stubby to express his joy.

Temmi stretched out his hand and Cush gave it a rapturous licking in return. The cage door was tied with string; using his father's old knife, Temmi cut through it and the door immediately fell open and Cush came tumbling out.

He gazed up at Temmi adoringly, his back half still waggling.

'Go, Cush,' whispered Temmi. 'Fly away—go back to Beog and the other bears.'

Cush bounded playfully around his feet. Across on the other side of the fire a wolf stirred.

Temmi knew for sure he was going to be caught now. But there was no reason for Cush to be caught with him. Not caring about the noise he made, he snatched up the little bear and flung him high into the air.

Cush hovered looking puzzled. Then, deciding this was only a game, he came gliding back down to earth.

That same moment a ferocious-looking wolf leapt through the flames of the fire, its pointed teeth snapping shut like a trap around Cush, even before Cush could touch the ground again.

A shout ripped out of Temmi—then men and wolves came running.

## Chapter Five

Tin Nose led them, looking startlingly different in a silver nose that was as pointed as a dagger. He bore down upon Frostbite giving such a bellow that everyone else stood still. Then, with the flat of his sword still in its scabbard, he struck the wolf a heavy blow across his back. Frostbite's mouth sprang open to yelp and a white ball of fur and feathers dropped to the ground.

Temmi scooped Cush up, holding him tenderly in his arms. Cush, wet with wolf-spit, trembled and whimpered, and one of his wings trailed at an angle like a broken fan, unable to close on his back as neatly as the other. Temmi touched it and Cush squealed with pain.

Tin Nose hovered over them like a storm about to break, his drawn sword flashing in his hand. 'I ought to kill you here and now for the trouble you've caused,' he said, fighting back his rage.

Although afraid, Temmi met his glare full on. 'This is your fault!' he shouted. 'You shouldn't have killed Pasha and taken Cush—'

He cringed as Tin Nose lifted his sword high above his head, but then saw Tin Nose pause as he noticed how trustingly Cush nestled in his arms. Slowly the sword went back to Tin Nose's side.

'Can you mend the creature's wing, boy?' he demanded gruffly. 'A flying bear that does not fly will be no use to the Witch's daughter and may cost me dear.'

'I can bind it if you give me the things I need,' said Temmi coldly. 'And I don't do it for you, but for Cush.'

Tin Nose had some men bring strips of blanket for bandages and sent others to find twigs for splints. He stood at a distance, his arms folded, watching impatiently as Temmi gently closed Cush's damaged wing to his body and tied it into place.

Cush was very frightened until he realized that

Temmi was trying to help him and, except for a whimper now and again, lay perfectly still. However, afterwards, when both wings were tied together, he was unable to understand why they wouldn't open when he tried. He shot Temmi a questioning look.

'It's for your own good, Cush,' explained Temmi, patting him.

Cush half-heartedly wagged his tail, still not entirely convinced.

Tin Nose then ordered Temmi to put Cush back into his cage. Temmi hated doing this as much as he hated Tin Nose for ordering it, but he had no other choice.

Once the cage door was secured, Temmi found himself dragged across to one of the snow burrows and bundled inside it.

Tin Nose roared for Frostbite.

The wolf slunk across, low-bellied, casting his master sulky, simmering looks. Tin Nose grabbed his scruff and thrust him down beside Temmi saying, 'If the boy tries to escape in the night, he is yours to devour in as many bites as you please.'

Frostbite turned his head, his damp breath panting over Temmi's face.

'Rrrr . . .'

He showed every pointed tooth and fang; and Temmi wondered if this was how a wolf laughed.

It felt as if he had only been asleep for a few minutes before a general stirring around Temmi awoke him. He opened his eyes. It was still completely dark, but the men were breaking up camp and the wolves were busily marking the place before moving on.

Temmi ran across and peered into Cush's cage. The bear appeared utterly miserable, but otherwise no worse than yesterday.

Two men approached and, ignoring the boy's pleas to be careful, slotted a pair of poles through the cage and lifted it off the ground. Cush turned restlessly in his confined space, wondering how it was he was flying when his wings didn't beat.

'Don't worry, Cush, I'll walk alongside you,' whispered Temmi reassuringly.

Minutes later the party set off, with no sign of daylight in the sky and flurries of snow blowing into their eyes. It was the start of a long, difficult journey and always in snow: with it either heaped-up so deeply they had to dig through it, or thickening the air as a howling blizzard. And overshadowing them and stretching never-endingly into the distance loomed ranks of unnamed mountains, gale-blasted snow streaming vertically from each shining peak.

At night-time, when they made camp, Temmi would gaze up through the blue half-light and believe that the mountains were powdery giants: certainly they were watchful giants, and perhaps malicious ones too. Once, the sleeping company narrowly missed being swept away by an avalanche. The sound of it was the roar of a mountain brought to its knees—the sound you will hear when the world finally ends.

And, as with the ever-present snow and mountains, so it was with the bitter, bone-gnawing cold. Like the Witch's men, Temmi's skin gradually took on a grey hue, his lips turned grey and his eyes turned grey. His teeth no longer chattered and he managed to use his unfeeling hands and feet. And when he saw that his finger-nails were black with cold, he shrugged and accepted this for the way things are in the High Witchlands. But really it was the cold which stopped him from caring for anything—except Cush.

For much of the time Temmi moved as if in a dream, the frozen spindrift pulling at his heels and the endless snowy wastes emptying his mind, making him only aware of one foot going down after the other, stumbling into the deep boot-holes of the man who went before him. Even the wolves were less lively now, slinking along close beside the men, their coats weighed down with dirty ice. Without smells the land was as dead to them as it was for Temmi.

Then, eight days after they set out to reach it, they finally arrived at the Witch's castle. Despite his dullness, his hearty sickness of all things snow and ice, Temmi stirred as if awakening from a deep sleep and stared in disbelief.

The castle was a jewel set in gardens of perfect snow, and was quite unlike any building he had ever seen before—or any building he had ever imagined possible. Built entirely from a single block of ice, it resembled a gigantic quartz crystal—that is to say, like an explosion of water that instantly freezes. Its numerous towers of varying height thrust out in all directions and leaned at different angles; and there were no windows or visible entrances in any of its massive crystal walls.

Arriving at its foot, they gathered before a deep ravine. Tin Nose immediately cupped his hands to his mouth and shouted above the droning wind, 'Lord Thurbolt commands you to open!'

Whereupon a slab of ice silently slid out from

the base of the wall, crossing the ravine to form a bridge. At the same time a rectangular ice door opened above it, allowing the party to cross and enter.

Speechless with awe, Temmi followed the others inside.

## Chapter Six

The ice door closed behind them without a sound and, although Temmi searched very carefully, he was unable to find an edge or evidence of hinges. The door had become part of the glassy wall once more. Around him the Witch's men were no longer tired slouchers, but had pulled back their shoulders, suddenly straight and alert. Stepping into line they formed a marching column.

Temmi hung close to Cush's cage, marvelling at everything he saw. The translucent walls of the corridor were smooth ice, allowing the light to filter through in shifting tones of blue, gold, and pink. Underfoot, unblemished snow made a carpet of equal depth throughout; and the ceiling was jagged with icicles.

If one were to fall, thought Temmi, it would pierce a man like a spear. Walking beneath such a ceiling was rather like walking into a shark's mouth and waiting at any moment for it to snap shut.

Temmi (a little fish in such circumstances) cowered his head and Cush sniffed the air uneasily.

The corridor wound on and on, never once passing a door—or visible door—and never once coming upon another's footprints in the glittering snow. Presently they reached a grand staircase with columns of huge barley-sugar twisted icicles, and snow-drifts poised one upon another to form a delicate banister.

At the top of the stairs, peering down at them, stood a thin woman in palest blue. She stood perfectly still, clutching her hands before her. Her hair was twisted into three severe conical horns on the top of her head, and she wore icicle jewellery about her throat and wrists; and icicles hung like pendants from her ears. She looked as if she had been frozen to the spot; and Temmi shivered just to see her, more so because her lips were blue and her skin so white as to appear bloodless.

On reaching the top step, Tin Nose went forward, briefly kissing her on the cheek. Her expression remained aloof.

'Husband,' she murmured, staring ahead with unfocused eyes.

'My Lady Sybia,' he replied. 'Are you well?'

She nodded slowly. 'But I fear the old Queen is failing fast. She asked for you to be brought to her as soon as you arrived.'

'Then take us to her at once.'

Lady Sybia turned and led them down an ice corridor, barely leaving a mark on the snow carpet, her light, wispy gown floating about her. Studying her close to, Temmi realized that her lips and finger nails were not blue with paint and varnish, but from the bitter cold; and her jewellery gently tinkled as she moved, making the sound a chandelier makes when caught by a breeze.

Suddenly a wild shriek arose from behind. The company halted and Lady Sybia frowned as a bare-footed girl, her hair fashioned into points like icicles, came racing up. The men immediately knelt, resting their foreheads against their spear-shafts.

'Princess Agna,' chided Lady Sybia, 'how many more times do I have to tell you not to run? Running produces heat and heat is an abomination.'

Princess Agna wasn't listening. 'Is that him? Is that my flying bear?' she asked, jumping up and down and clapping her hands in delight. She was so noisy that Cush growled softly at her from the back of his cage.

'Tell it to be silent!' ordered the girl, her mouth suddenly becoming firm.

'If you stood still and stopped shouting,' said Temmi, 'Cush wouldn't growl so.'

Lady Sybia shot him a sharp glance and Princess Agna stood open-mouthed. It was clear nobody ever spoke to her in such a direct way.

'Tin Nose, why have you brought me another pet dwarf?' she cried, glancing across at Temmi. 'I've all the dwarfs I can play with already: and they're so bad-tempered and they don't wash and they always reek of their horrible pipe-tobacco. I don't want any more smelly old dwarfs.'

'Forgive me, Princess, he is not a dwarf,' replied Tin Nose diffidently. 'He is a boy.'

'A *boy*?' Princess Agna looked puzzled. 'Do you mean an ungrown man?'

'Yes, Princess. Unlike your dwarfs he will one day grow as big as me.'

'How tiresome and untidy. He will look out of

place amongst my other dwarfs. Why did you bring him?'

'It was necessary, Princess. The flying bear was . . . injured. The boy takes care of it.'

Remembering the bear, Princess Agna grew excited once more. 'Take him from the cage and let me see him properly.'

'Do it, boy,' snarled Tin Nose.

Reluctantly Temmi opened the cage. 'Come on, Cush,' he whispered. 'Nobody will hurt you—not while *I'm* here.' He pointedly addressed his remark at the girl.

Yet when she at last had Cush in her arms, Princess Agna held him with great awkwardness. She squeezed him. The bear panicked and began to struggle. Stepping forward, Temmi quickly snatched him back and stroked him until he was calm again.

'The bear is bad-tempered and must be beaten!' announced the Princess. 'He must have his fur trimmed. It is making him too hot and irritable.'

Lady Sybia touched the Princess's shoulder with fingers as long and elegant as icicles. 'We can attend to these matters later, Princess,' she said. 'But your royal mother first commands us to attend her.'

Temmi held Cush as they proceeded through

the castle. The corridor grew higher and wider, with ice columns running down the middle and snow crisp upon the floor.

Then Lady Sybia stopped and reached out her hand, gently touching the frost-marbled wall with her fingertips. At once a huge slab of ice swung open and the company entered the Witch's chamber, wolves and all, their heads held low in respect for the dying Queen.

Temmi entered, feeling more than a little uneasy. To be in the presence of a queen was daunting enough, but a queen who was also a witch! This gave him good reason to stand well back in the shadows.

The Queen's bed dominated the chamber. It was a block of softly glowing ice with an ice post shining at each corner. Draped from the posts were curtains of lace, made entirely of snowflakes, like the web of a snow spider. Behind them, Haggoth, Witch-Queen of the High Witchlands, appeared very old and frail. Her nose was long and pointed while the rest of her face was sunken and wrinkled. From her chin sprouted whiskers.

The men dropped to their knees and the wolves lay at the foot of her bed.

The witch spoke.

'Lady Sybia . . . has your husband finally returned?'

Her voice sent a shiver through Temmi, not because it was frightening, but because it was so thin and brittle and utterly cold.

Lady Sybia glided forward. 'Yes,' she breathed. 'He is here.'

'Tell him to step into the light so I may see him.'

Tin Nose obeyed, kneeling beside the bed. The Witch's claw of a hand reached out tremblingly until it rested on his head.

'You have returned safely, Lord Thurbolt. You have brought the flying bear and presented it to Princess Agna?'

'Yes, majesty.'

Haggoth sighed. 'Good. Then you have arrived in time for my death.'

'No!' screamed Princess Agna. 'I will not listen to such talk. You are a witch and can make yourself better. You will never die!'

As weak as she was, Haggoth turned to her with a terrible stare. 'Child—get rid of that melt water from your eyes or get out of my presence for ever! You shall be a queen soon. Your heart must be ice. Always *ice*!'

The Princess drew in her breath and her tears,

freezing on her face, dropped sparkling to the ground.

'She is raw and inexperienced,' sighed the Witch wearily. 'You and Lady Sybia must bring her up in my place, Thurbolt. When she is twelve give her my wand and teach her the magic of ice . . . the enchantment of snow . . . the bewitchment of frost. Make her love the Cold as much as I have, in all its cruelty and beauty.'

Tin Nose bowed low. 'I promise,' he said.

'And just as importantly, Thurbolt,' continued the Witch, a hardening edge to her voice, 'you must protect her from the evils of *warmth*. Warmth brings corruption and change. It makes that which is solid melt away into nothing. It pollutes the whiteness and turns men into dependent weaklings. It is the opposite of all we love, and possesses its own magic which defies our control. Remember this, Thurbolt. Remember it always.'

'*Always*, majesty.'

The claw lifted from his head. The Queen's eyes began to close. 'Go now. Leave me in peace to listen to the sweet murmurings of the ice.'

The men rose, bowed, and went out as silently as ghosts. The wolves crawled after them, their bellies touching the floor. At the door Temmi glanced back. The foot and pawprints were slowly disappearing from the snow, leaving it smooth and white once more.

The corridor seemed dazzling after the dimness of the Witch's bedchamber. The men led the wolves away to be fed. Lady Sybia turned to Princess Agna and with a cold smile said, 'Take your boy and bear to the nursery, Princess. I must speak with my husband.'

'Come on, boy,' said the Princess to Temmi. 'I will show you the dwarfs and where you will live.'

'Be sure not to run, Princess,' Lady Sybia called after her. 'You don't want to break out in an unhealthy pink flush.'

'I shall do whatever I please,' muttered the Princess under her breath.

## Chapter Seven

Princess Agna's nursery occupied one of the many leaning towers, with walls and floors coming together at a sharp angle, the grain in the ice running in different directions. Much of the tower was crooked staircase and featureless corridor, while the rest was empty rooms, one leading into the next until at last they reached the Princess's bedroom.

The lofty room had scarce few pieces of furniture, but what it did have was suitably grand and carved from ice. To Temmi's surprise, the Princess's bed was a snow-drift which reminded him of a frozen wave, its sparkling crest about to tumble. It was supported by a number of snowmen standing shoulder to shoulder, and a ladder, held by a kneeling snowman, was the only means of climbing in.

Across, on the opposite side of the room, the ice wall had been carved into deep shelves. On the shelves like living toys were the Princess's pet dwarfs. A couple sat playing cards, one chewed a long-stemmed pipe, another snoozed, and the last was carving a small block of ice into a frost flower.

Temmi stared, having never seen a dwarf before, because they weren't at all like small men. They were hairy, stocky creatures, with old men's faces. They had broad heads and tiny ears, wide mouths and small noses. Only one of them was clean shaven.

They were also extremely noisy, squabbling about the cards or being in each other's way; and they all elbowed the sleeper if he snored. Temmi thought they must enjoy squabbling because there were plenty of empty shelves where they could go to escape each other, only they seemed not to want to.

None of the dwarfs noticed them arrive until the Princess screamed at them to be silent.

They blinked down at her, screwing up their tiny eyes; their stares jumping from the girl to the boy to the bear in his arms.

'Come down,' ordered the Princess.

The dwarfs clumsily climbed off their shelf and came padding over. Temmi smiled once or twice at them, but received only the most unfriendly scowls in return.

The girl introduced her pets. The bearded dwarfs were Wormlugs, Crumbtoot, Mudsniff, and Flywick. The beardless one was called Kobble. Then Temmi was introduced to them in a manner almost dismissive.

'Begging your pardon, Princess,' said Wormlugs, working up his shoulders. 'But he's not a *proper* dwarf. He's likely to grow lanky on you and try to boss us around.'

'Yes,' agreed Flywick. 'Big bosses little. That's the law of the world.'

'I'm not a bully,' said Temmi fiercely.

'It speaks!' cried Mudsniff, genuinely amazed.

'But it's still not a proper dwarf,' grumbled Wormlugs. 'Besides, there's no room on the shelves for him.'

Temmi saw this was clearly untrue, but said nothing. He did not like the idea of being considered a pet and living on a shelf!

'The boy is my bear-keeper,' explained Princess Agna loftily. 'He and the bear must have a room

45

of their own; and when the bear is well again he shall sleep at the bottom of my bed, and the boy can be given some other job at the palace—like ice polishing.'

This pleased the dwarfs no end and they nodded at each other, although Temmi was far less happy to hear his future so firmly decided for him.

'Now,' continued the Princess, 'if we don't soon play a game the day will be totally wasted.'

'What about dwarf skittles?' shyly suggested Kobble the beardless dwarf. 'We used to play that all the time.'

The four other dwarfs glowered at him for daring to make a remark.

'That is . . . ' said Kobble weakly, 'if you feel that you . . . want to, Princess.'

The girl stood in the attitude of thinking, her expression solemn. 'Yes,' she finally decided. '*Dwarf skittles*. I'd forgotten it was my favourite game and I order you to play it with me *now*.'

When she turned her back, the four other dwarfs pinched Kobble hard. Kobble thrust his fingers into his mouth to stop a cry coming out; and then Wormlugs glared at Temmi before pinching *him* for good measure too. It was just as hard as the pinch he gave Kobble, right at the top of his arm.

Temmi quickly learnt what expert pinchers dwarfs can be.

The game of dwarf skittles was played along an ice-floored corridor. The rules were simple enough to be gathered at a glance. In fact they were the same as in ordinary skittles, the only difference being that the wooden pins were replaced by living dwarfs; and the Princess took aim at their shins with a heavy wooden ball. When the ball hit a dwarf he was supposed to lie down. But dwarfs, as well as being first-rate pinchers, were also champion cheats and extraordinarily bad losers. Temmi smiled as he watched them inch this way or that from the path of the ball, or simply deny that it struck them at all. The Princess screamed with rage, threatening all manner of horrible tortures, but to no avail.

'Such a hot-tempered one,' Wormlugs was heard to mutter into his beard.

Princess Agna flared up again. 'Bad language! Bad language, Wormlugs! I shall tell Lady Sybia and she'll hang you by your thumbs from the roof of the wolf house.'

Temmi realized it was the word *hot* she had taken violent exception to.

47

Mercifully a deep tolling bell put an end to all threats and squabbles.

'Good,' said Crumbtoot brightening. 'Dinner time. I'm starving.'

The dwarfs and the Princess hurried down to dinner in a noisy throng. Temmi followed holding a sleeping Cush. As he went along Kobble sidled up to him and tugged his sleeve. 'You mustn't mind us dwarfs,' he said, 'we're not really so bad once you get to know us.'

Temmi was not convinced. 'Do dwarfs always pinch as hard?' he asked.

'Oh yes,' replied Kobble proudly. 'As Wormlugs says, "Big bosses little, old bosses young". I'm the smallest and youngest dwarf, you see.'

'Huh, I suppose Wormlugs is the biggest and oldest?'

Kobble's face lightened with surprise. 'Why yes. How did you guess?'

'It wasn't difficult.'

'But he's also the bravest too,' Kobble went on. 'He's always tormenting Frostbite and working him into a rage. They're deadly enemies, you see.' He glanced down at Cush peacefully asleep in Temmi's arms. 'Your bear looks much more friendly than any of the Witch's wolves. Do you think . . . that is . . . can I stroke—'

'Kobble!' snarled Wormlugs suddenly turning around and catching him. 'What have you to talk about with a *b-oy*? Come away to your own kind. He may be a spy.'

'I . . . I better go,' mumbled Kobble, 'Wormlugs is—'

'The biggest and the oldest,' finished Temmi sarcastically.

By this time they had entered the great hall, which lay at the very heart of the castle. Tables and benches were carved from ice and giant snowflakes hung from the domed ceiling. At the high table was a throne of clear ice—empty, of course, because the Witch-Queen was dying. On one side of it sat Tin Nose, with Lady Sybia on the other. Princess Agna, Temmi, Cush, and the dwarfs clustered about the end of the table where manners were altogether more free and easy.

Below them sat the Witch's men, the wolves passing unrestricted amongst them, finding food where they could.

Wormlugs tossed a bone to Frostbite and when the wolf dived for it, Wormlugs quickly reeled it back, laughing as he did so: the bone was tied to a piece of string.

'Rarrr!' Frostbite's yellow eyes glared at Wormlugs with undisguised hatred.

'One day, dwarf, you will torment my wolf once too often,' murmured Tin Nose calmly, 'and then you will wish you hadn't.' Meaningfully he tapped his false nose, which tonight was of gold with a garnet set at the end—like an ugly boil, thought Temmi.

The food arrived with noise and clamour and eagerly Temmi awaited it, until he saw it was meat—blood-red meat not the slightest bit cooked, and then he was appalled. Why, not even on the trail to the castle had he ever been forced to eat raw meat. And now the memory of those meagre rations of dried fish and tasteless biscuits that Tin Nose doled out every evening grew much less unpleasant when compared to dinner at the Witch's table.

The meal progressed and Temmi quickly decided that perhaps worse than the food itself was having to watch others who considered it delicious. In open-mouthed horror he saw Princess Agna seize up the meat in her neat little hands and begin taking savage bites. Soon her face and fingers were red and sticky with blood. And finally done, she casually tossed the picked bone away only to snatch more meat from the plate.

'Don't you want any?' she asked Temmi through gnawing bites.

'No, Princess,' he muttered weakly. 'You can have my share if you like.'

Although Temmi had no stomach for raw meat himself, he tried feeding a little to Cush. But even Cush found it not to his liking and chewed with a distasteful expression, as if ready to spit it out. Flying bears are fish eaters in the wild and the raw meat seemed strange to Cush: yet he was so hungry he ate all that Temmi offered him.

Then a dish of uncooked vegetables was slammed down and the waiting dwarfs pounced upon it. In the scramble a hunk of swede rolled Temmi's way and he snatched it up and gobbled it down. However, when he tried to take something else from the dish, Wormlugs's rucked-up shoulders blocked him. Noticing this, Kobble gave Temmi a carrot, passing it to him under the table. Yet no sooner was it in Temmi's hand than Wormlugs snatched it back.

Temmi was so angry he retaliated in the way a dwarf best understood—with a savage pinch, right between his shoulder blades. Wormlugs gave an unnecessarily loud howl and leapt to his feet.

'Dwarf-slayer!' he bawled.

'Thief!' returned Temmi.

Seconds later they were fighting, sending plates

and dishes clattering to the floor. The fight had hardly begun before Tin Nose rushed over and tore them apart. The entire hall was silent and watching.

'Such behaviour before a princess,' hissed Lady Sybia. 'Mark me, husband, that boy will bring nothing but trouble.'

Tin Nose drew his sword.

'Put that away, Tin Nose!' ordered Princess Agna, her face as bloody as a feeding tiger's and her eyes blazing.

Tin Nose hesitated. 'One day soon, Princess, you will be Queen,' he said in a soft purring growl. 'You should remember to keep about you only those whose presence is fit.'

'And *you* should remember that when *I* am Queen *I* shall give the commands, not *you*, Tin Nose.'

The Princess took another slab of meat and, without turning her head, casually ordered the guards to take the two brawlers from the table. 'Let them go hungry. That shall be their punishment,' she said.

Temmi was glad it was left for her to decide for, as he and Wormlugs were marched away, he caught the look on Tin Nose's face as he reluctantly re-sheathed his sword.

## Chapter Eight

That night Temmi lay shivering under a greasy wolf pelt on the floor of his ice cell next to the Princess's bedroom. He was unable to sleep, and cold and hunger made his misery all the more unbearable. Despite trying not to, his thoughts kept flying back to his father, bringing with them memories of his village and lake. He imagined he could smell freshly-caught fish baking in the fire and warm bread, crusty and good. Tear followed tear down his cheeks until Cush's fur grew quite damp in the place where he rested his head.

All around them the castle was still. Still but not silent, for the ice softly creaked and groaned under its own bulk, speaking the secret language of ice.

But then, as Temmi listened, he heard the unmistakable sound of a door opening. It was the door adjoining the Princess's bedroom; and judging by the great effort being taken, he was not meant to hear it at all. Voices whispered. Cush stirred.

'Hush,' Temmi whispered to him. 'It's those sneaky dwarfs.'

Temmi and Cush listened intently, wondering what was going on. At first Temmi thought that, under Wormlugs's persuading, the dwarfs had come to harm him. But he soon dismissed this idea as the dwarfs took care to avoid him, creeping by on some other secret business of their own.

The snow crunched ever so slightly beneath the dwarfs' sealskin boots, but most noise was made by Wormlugs telling his fellows to be quiet.

Reaching the far wall they pushed open the door and stole out into the passageway. Then the door swished to behind them.

Intrigued, Temmi jumped up. Cush bounded up with him, but Temmi shook his head. 'No, Cush. You stay here—you can stand guard.'

Cush yawned. It was obvious he'd be asleep in a minute or two. Temmi gave him a friendly pat and left.

Following the dwarfs' footprints, Temmi found the concealed door. He saw everything perfectly clearly, for moonlight streamed through the ice castle making the walls shimmer a ghostly blue.

Temmi pushed open the door and peered through. The passageway outside was empty and the dwarfs' footprints were fast fading in the snow. Quickly he hurried after them. The footprints ended abruptly at a blank wall. Temmi touched it and a door opened for him. Behind it lay, not another empty chamber as he expected, but a circular stairway going down as deeply as a well.

If Temmi hesitated it was only for a moment, then he started the downward climb determined to discover the dwarfs' secret. The stairs went on twisting beneath him, and almost without his realizing the ice turned into rock — then the light changed. No longer was it blue, powdery moonlight, but flickering orange firelight; and whereas the moonlight filtered down from above, the orange firelight sprang from below.

Knowing himself close to finding his answer,

Temmi cautiously approached the light which moved restlessly across the wet rock—now red, now yellow, now orange. Besides the light there was also smoke—wood-smoke—rising up the stairs like a chimney; and Temmi could hear sticks crackling as they burned. Then, catching low voices about the fire, he stood still listening to the dwarfs in conversation.

'Ahh, this is the warmest my toes have been all day,' he heard Mudsniff sigh contentedly. 'I'm sure my beard is frozen stiff enough to snap from my chin as cleanly as an icicle.'

'You'd look like Kobble if it does,' said Crumbtoot.

Gruff dwarfish laughter broke out at this.

Peering around the bottom of the stairway, Temmi saw a good fire burning well, sending up sparks to the roof of a cave. The dwarfs sat close to the flames, their faces shining in the fierce orange light.

As he continued watching, Temmi saw Wormlugs take up a shovel which had been crudely hammered into a frying-pan shape. This set the other dwarfs busily emptying their pockets, taking out the pieces of raw meat they had stolen at dinner time and arranging them carefully in the pan for frying.

'Oldest and biggest gets bestest and mostest,' declared Wormlugs greedily.

'Why are your pieces of meat always covered in fluff, Kobble?' complained Flywick.

'Give him a good pinch,' said Wormlugs. 'That'll wake his ideas.'

'You leave him be!' cried Temmi, suddenly stepping from the shadows.

The dwarfs froze in surprise. In fact at that moment they resembled nothing so much as a gathering of gargoyles, and their gaping mouths might have been made that way for spouting rain-water. Had he not been so angry, Temmi probably would have laughed out loud at them.

'Kobble is the only decent one among you,' he shouted. 'None of you other dwarfs would share your food with me. You'd let me starve!'

Wormlugs picked up the frying-pan, which he had dropped into the flames at Temmi's appearance. The heated handle made him grimace.

'Told you he was the Witch's spy,' he said darkly. 'That pip-squeak, that halfling, that *pretend* dwarf.'

Kobble began to snivel, then Flywick started to cry setting off Crumbtoot and Mudsniff. Wormlugs fought against it, but he was pretty near to weeping himself and kept clearing his throat most unconvincingly.

'Why are you crying?' asked Temmi surprised.

'Because you will tell the Witch,' wailed Mudsniff, 'and she will nail our beards to the trees and leave us there for the crows.'

Setting aside the fact Kobble had no beard to be hoisted by, Temmi said, 'Tell her what?'

'Th-that we have l-lit a f-fire at the pa-palace, and to w-warm yourself by f-fire and to eat h-hot dinners are b-both a-against the l-law.'

'Against the law?'

'Punishable by death,' whispered Flywick.

Temmi paused to consider the number of times he must have broken the Witch's law. 'Well, I shan't tell her. Move up. Give me some room. Don't you think I hate being cold too?'

They stared at him in astonishment.

'I suppose we could make room,' said Crumbtoot hesitantly.

'And if you're cooking, I wouldn't mind a share of the meat,' said Temmi peering into the pan. 'Well fried, please—all the way through.'

'Boys are pretty much like dwarfs,' decided Kobble happily.

'Pretty much,' agreed Temmi.

The dwarfs threw more sticks on the fire

and the hot pan made the meat sizzle in its own juices, the smell growing more and more delicious until the meat was cooked and ready to be eaten.

They had no plates, but the flat stones that littered the cave did just as well; and Wormlugs was content to eat straight from the pan. Nobody spoke as they chewed, it was understood to be too serious a business to interrupt with idle chit-chat. The older dwarfs used their beards as napkins; Kobble and Temmi licked their fingers clean. Not a bit was wasted.

It was while they were finishing their supper that a bell began to toll, sounding loudly even deep underground.

Straight away Wormlugs leapt to his feet, his eyes slitted and suspicious.

'The warning bell!' he cried. 'The boy *is* a spy after all. He's betrayed us to the Witch!'

'No,' insisted Flywick. 'Why ring the bell when we might easily be arrested without half so much fuss? This is something bigger than dwarfs warming their beards by a fire.'

'Perhaps the castle is under attack?' suggested Kobble.

'Stupid—who'd dare attack the Witch?' growled Wormlugs giving him a sly pinch.

Temmi chewed his lip. 'Then there is only one possible answer,' he said gravely. 'The Witch has finally died.'

And they all looked at each other in wonder.

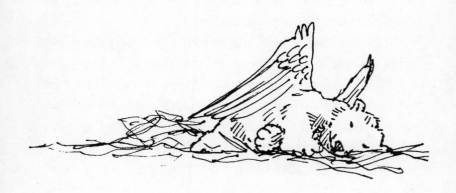

## Chapter Nine

By moonlight they carried the Witch's frail body out of the castle on a slab of ice: a bearer at each corner and one at each side. The Witch was dressed in sparkling white like a bride on her wedding day, for death was now her husband, the most lasting cold of all.

Behind the Witch came her people and her wolves, passing between shapeless heaps of snow.

At the head of the column the chief mourners were also dressed in white—Lady Sybia's veil cascading to her knees and through it only her blue lips were visible. Her husband, Tin Nose, wore his best ermine-trimmed cloak, and his silver nose had flaring nostrils that coiled back in deep

grooves. Beside him Princess Agna sobbed bitterly.

'Control, madam! Control!' Lady Sybia hissed at her from beneath her veil.

Further down the column, where the mourners wore simple white ribbons, the dwarfs were to be found; but Temmi and Cush were right at the back among the pot scourers and ice polishers, strange misshapen creatures who shuffled along in sacking tied up with string.

In the silence, Temmi caught snatches of fearful whispers.

'What will it be like having a girl rule over us?' hissed a voice to his side.

'Not a girl,' answered another voice, 'she is too young. The power will rest in Lord Thurbolt's hands, at least until the Princess is older.'

'But what if he gets a taste for power?'

'Hush, that is not our business. Let us see off the old Queen first.'

Handfuls of snow came on the wind, flecking hair and the wolves' ragged coats. A blizzard was stirring itself, some saying it was fitting that it should; others murmuring that it was the Witch's last gasp of magic. Nobody thought to hurry because of it; and at a stately pace they carried the Witch down to the river where her dragon boat had waited in readiness since the day she first fell ill.

Carefully the slab-bearers laid the Witch upon the deck before solemnly filing back across the gangplank. With his sword Tin Nose hacked through the mooring rope and the sail came down with a sound like a rug being shaken, revealing the Witch's insignia: the black snowflake that a thousand suns cannot melt.

Then, with everyone gathered to watch, the boat was caught by the current and smoothly moved away from the bank, out into the middle of the river.

The sight sent Agna wild with grief. She would have thrown herself into the water after it had not Tin Nose prevented her.

Snatching her hand free of his grasp she scrambled away, the wolves streaming after her, and all through the night they ran together, howling and raging at the moon.

## Chapter Ten

'The Queen is dead: Long live the Queen!'

This was a cry Temmi heard many times over the next few days. He started crooning it to Cush, and Cush, not knowing what it meant, simply wagged his tail affectionately.

But a great change was brought about by the death of the old Queen, Haggoth.

Returning to the castle at dawn, Agna amazed all the people she met, with her show of composure and aloofness. Those that saw her reported that, although her eyes were red, she shed no more tears. The wolves walked respectfully beside her; and in the passageways her men dropped to their knees, lowering their gaze.

She never returned to the nursery. Her dwarfs and other toys were forgotten. Temmi heard she had taken up residence in the royal apartments; and saw her only in the great hall presiding over feasts, dining on delicate morsels of raw meat. And if he looked too hard towards the high throne his eyes were dazzled by her frost crown. It was as if she had been lost to the radiance of ice, which naturally thrilled Lord Thurbolt and his wife.

'Majesty,' breathed Lady Sybia curtsying low. 'It chills my heart with gladness to see you make yourself in the image of your dear mother.'

Agna regarded her coldly. '*Her* law is *my* law. The ice shall not give an inch to the thaw. Serve me and see it is so.'

Lady Sybia trembled with pleasure. She was sure Agna would make a great queen, perhaps even greater than her mother.

The dwarfs quickly grew bored. They were so used to being pets of a princess that without their mistress they couldn't organize themselves to do anything except squabble: Wormlugs starting an argument if ever they were in need of one (which usually they weren't), while poor Kobble was pinched into silence the moment he opened his mouth. Quite honestly Temmi lost patience with them.

He much preferred to spend his time with Cush. Cush didn't argue about who had the most eyelashes, or who was able to hold his breath the longest, or who woke up first that morning. Cush was better company by far; and if his injured wing meant he was still unable to fly, well Temmi was content just having the little bear gambolling along beside him.

Each day, at some point, Temmi made sure he took Cush up on to the castle roof. The visit was worthwhile for the view alone, with towers sprouting out below them and soaring up behind like frozen rockets—and beyond lay the snowfields and the forest stretching as far as the mountains themselves. But there was another more serious reason for their visits.

Temmi knew that Cush had to learn the different winds that blew—because, to a flying bear, these are as vital as the ocean currents to whales and dolphins; each wind being as distinct as the colours of the rainbow. The north wind was black, the south wind yellowy-green, the east wind blue, and the west wind brown with orange tips; and the winds in between were shades of all the others.

One day, as Cush's wet, sniffy nose was

making itself acquainted with a purply-grey north-westerly, a voice spoke to Temmi.

He spun round at once and there was Agna. She was standing on a slightly higher roof, barefoot in the snow. For a moment Temmi forgot she was Queen of the High Witchlands and saw only a small thing swamped in grown-ups' clothing. But then he remembered who she had become and bowed low, allowing Cush to jump up into his arms. The cub was unsure whether to growl or wag his tail.

Agna stared at him. 'The bear—doesn't he fly yet?'

Temmi gave Cush a gentle stroke, as if he might take offence at the remark. 'No, Majesty. His wing needs time to mend still.'

'Oh.' Agna made the empty sound and glanced about her, as if never really interested in the first place.

'But he is getting stronger, thank you, Majesty.'

'Oh?'

'And eating more fish.'

'Indeed?'

'Soon I hope he will be flying again.'

'Yes.'

'Would . . . would you care to stroke him, Majesty?'

'*No* . . . no, thank you.'

An awkward silence fell between them. Temmi smiled. He half expected Agna to burst out laughing at any moment and stop this pretence of being the grand royal.

But Agna only tilted her head and looked at him puzzled. 'Why do you smile?'

'Oh, nothing, Majesty. I was just thinking, Cush and I often come here, but we have never seen you on the roofs before.'

'That is because I have been exploring,' she said airily. 'It is my first task as Queen to find every room in my castle, then it has no secrets to use against me.' Suddenly her voice grew low and confiding. 'But listen, Temmi, I have seen so many things you wouldn't believe. Only this morning I . . . Oh, but naturally I can't tell you—I am Queen, you understand, and such sights are for the Queen's eyes only.'

Temmi thought she had almost forgotten about the crown upon her head and become just like any ordinary girl who was bursting to tell her news. He was right. Agna longed to tell him about the room that held the hide of a frost dragon, and the room with thousands of brightly jewelled fish frozen into the walls. Then there was the room where the yellow ice was more ancient

69

than the land, and the room with more ways in than out, which housed the old Witch's three great books of magic: one that governed the snow, one that governed the frost, and one that governed the ice.

'I'm sure you do the right thing, Majesty,' replied Temmi, who couldn't resist adding, 'Why, the mysteries of the castle aren't for the likes of a humble bear-keeper and fisherman's son.'

He thought she would recognize the gentle teasing and manage a smile—if only a little one. But when he looked across he saw Agna wasn't paying him the slightest attention at all.

'What's that noise?' she demanded.

Becoming once more royal and aloof she moved to the battlements and peered down. Temmi, holding Cush, followed but kept a pace behind. Below them on the snow plains he saw the five dwarfs returning from the forest. And the prospect of a warm fire built with the wood they brought made them less quarrelsome and better tempered. As Agna and Temmi watched, they laughed at Kobble as he threw himself into the snow—and it was their undignified honks, howls, and hee-haws that Agna had heard.

Temmi grew concerned. Hadn't he warned Wormlugs to take more care? Before, when they had a Princess to amuse, the dwarfs made do by smuggling in a few twigs at a time. But lately, with no one to question their comings and goings, they'd become dangerously open about what they did, even now dragging a heavy log behind them.

'Why do they laugh?' asked Agna irritably. 'Don't they know laughter is a weakness arising from unnecessary warmth of feeling?'

Temmi thought, you're just repeating the words that Tin Nose and his wife put into your head, but he said, 'Oh, you know how the dwarfs are, Majesty. Did you hear of Wormlugs's latest trick he played on Lord Thurbolt's wolf? Oh— and I nearly forgot to tell you, Cush has learnt to walk on his back legs, shall I sh—'

'And why are they bringing that filthy log into my castle? What can they possibly need it for?'

Before Temmi could think up a convincing explanation she murmured to herself, 'If those dwarfs are up to any mischief I shall find out. The castle has no secrets from its Queen.'

In their cave deep beneath the cellars of the ice castle, the dwarfs had gathered a good store of fuel. Rarely, if ever, was the fire allowed to go out now, and if it was low they quickly built it up again with twigs and logs. They spent many hours around it, hating the times they had to leave and go out into the cold.

Temmi did his best, he tried to warn them of the risk they took: but even he was drawn to the warmth of the fireside more often than he should have been.

And so it was that they were all gathered there, spreading their hands to the flames, when Queen Agna came down the twisting stairway and caught them.

'Blasphemy of blasphemies!' she screamed. 'How dare you bring this evil into the house of the Witch-Queen? You shall pay for this outrage— every one of you! You shall pay with your lives!'

The dwarfs immediately fell to their knees, whimpering and moaning and begging for mercy. Temmi, however, grew angry. Before him was no queen in a rage, but a girl—a rather small girl—in a tantrum.

'How can you be so afraid?' he cried, turning to the dwarfs; and determined to show them that what he saw was the truer picture, he ran over, seized Agna's ice cold wrist and dragged her towards the fire.

'How dare you!' she shrieked. 'How dare you lay hands on the Queen of the High Witchlands!'

'Oh be quiet, you . . . you . . . great spoilt baby!' blurted out Temmi, shocking the dwarfs as much as Agna herself.

'What can you be thinking of, boy?' hissed Wormlugs. 'You'll only make matters worse for us all. You'll only make our deaths more terrible.'

But Temmi was in no mood to listen. He shoved Agna down onto one of the large stones they used as seats and stood aside so she could feel the fire's strength.

'Torture! Torture!' she screamed. The dwarfs covered their ears and rolled into balls like hedgehogs.

'Of course it's not torture,' sneered Temmi. 'You only believe that because you were told it was true. Learn for yourself. The fire's warmth is actually kind.'

'I'm dying—you're killing me,' she cried, although her struggles were becoming less and less. 'See, I shake all over—I have caught a deadly disease.'

Temmi smiled. 'It is called shivering,' he explained patiently, as if to a very young child. 'And you're shivering because you've never realized just exactly how cold you were before.'

Agna fell silent. Soon the shivering bouts

73

stopped and she reached out her hands to the fire in wonder.

'Ah—ah, not too close,' warned Temmi, 'or the flames really will hurt you.'

At their feet the dwarfs slowly uncurled and sat up, staring at Agna in utter bewilderment. A rosiness was just appearing in the girl's cheeks, making her look less severe—and some might say pleasant.

Kobble smiled at the transformation. But when Agna tried a warm smile back, she was unsure which way her mouth should move (it is something others do without thinking, but she would have to learn).

As her body thawed, so did her thoughts. She began to recall a time and place outside the ice castle. But it was all so confusing—and frightening too, her mind swelling with colours and the echo of distant voices.

Suddenly and firmly her duty to the Cold blocked out all these things and she snatched back her hands.

'What am I doing?' she cried in disbelief. 'The frost crown is melting!' And she fled to the stairs, scrambling up them, the crown crooked and misshapen upon her head.

The dwarfs watched her go with gasps of dismay.

'Now she will send for the guards and they will kill us,' groaned Mudsniff.

'I don't think so,' said Temmi confidently, reaching out to the flames once more. 'If they kill us for breaking the law they must also kill the Queen. After all, hasn't she just warmed herself before our fire?'

The dwarfs knew this to be the case. The law was greater than the one who administers it.

Wormlugs softly chuckled and, casting the boy an admiring look, said, 'Oh, you're a crafty one all right.'

## Chapter Eleven

As the affairs of dwarfs and humans took their various twists and turns, Cush seemed to improve by the day. New feathers sprouted in place of the damaged ones and gradually his injured wing regained its full strength, until Temmi no longer saw a need to bind it, encouraging the bear to exercise both wings as much as possible with bouts of vigorous flapping. But because Cush had grown used to living among creatures who stayed firmly on the ground, he forgot that he could fly. The only answer, Temmi realized, was to teach him.

Thereafter it became a common sight to see Temmi take the bear out of the castle to instruct him on the finer points of flight. Of course, had Pasha been alive she would have done as much herself, the only difference being that Pasha would have been passing on something she knew, while Temmi, who madly flapped his arms until they ached, achieved nothing more than a sense of his own foolishness. The trouble was Cush had become lazy, and every time Temmi threw him up into the air he simply glided back to earth . . . and stayed there. It was all so frustrating.

'Cush! You have turned into a floppy old sag bear,' Temmi would shout at the end of each lesson.

Cush's reply, as always, was to hang out his tongue and pant happily.

In the end Temmi asked the dwarfs to help him. They grumbled but agreed. Now, whenever Cush was airborne, they refused to let him land, clapping their hands and shooing him back into the sky. It made quite a comical scene, with dwarfs running into each other or suddenly blundering into waist-deep snow.

By and by Cush realized he *was* a flying bear after all and took great delight in the fact, never ever walking if he could use his wings instead. Even in the castle he constantly buzzed around Temmi's head, nuzzling his neck or licking his face.

But the more pleased with himself Cush became the more gloomy grew Temmi.

He reached up and tickled Cush's belly. 'You don't deserve to be a prisoner here, Cush,' he said softly. 'When you are bigger and stronger I promise I shall give you your freedom.' He blinked back a tear. 'As for me, I will probably end my days as an ice-polisher—a slave of the Witch-Queen for ever.'

Fish.

That was the other great thing in their lives.

*Fish.*

No sooner was Cush flying again than his appetite trebled. He awoke in the night yowling for fish, and if Temmi had none to give him he covered his head with a wing and sulked. Yet it was rare for Cush to go hungry and the nursery floor was so strewn with fish heads and bones, that even Wormlugs complained of the stink.

Once, perhaps twice, a day, Temmi took Cush to the river to hunt, the sight never failing to thrill him. First, the long dive with wing tips nearly touching—then the smallest of splashes— speedily followed by the graceful climb into the sky, a trout squirming between Cush's front paws. Often Temmi ran a line of his own, but the river was so full of fish that, as a fisherman's son, he found them almost embarrassingly easy to catch (not that anyone else fished there, the river and the things that lived in it were considered unlucky at the castle).

Returning home one day with a catch so heavy it had to be dragged on a string behind him (each fish tail chewed ragged by Cush), Temmi spied Tin Nose and his wife deep in conversation on the forest track.

Tin Nose was upon a sleigh roped to four pairs of wolves, with Frostbite their front runner. Lady Sybia sat side-saddle on a motionless white elk.

'What can they be up to so far away from the castle?' wondered Temmi, suddenly curious to find out.

He beckoned Cush down into his arms and crept through the trees, until he reached a snow-drift where he could hide and listen.

'Well, tell me what exactly these worries are,' he heard Tin Nose demand.

Lady Sybia slowly wound the reins around her cold, bloodless hands. 'They are mostly feelings, husband, but I do truly believe our Queen is no longer of the Cold.'

'This is serious, lady. You need evidence for what you say.'

Lady Sybia's gaze remained on the frost fire of her rings. 'Very well . . . She has demanded extra furs on her bed and dresses indecently warm. She balks at her food and has actually asked me whether meat would not taste better *cooked*.'

'What did you tell her?'

She glared up at him. 'The truth of course! That cooked meat is poisonous.'

'Is there anything else?' asked Tin Nose gravely.

'Yes . . . Have you noticed her complexion is no longer the healthy white it was? And yesterday I caught her rubbing her hands together.'

'Did you not ask her why?'

'Of course,' snapped his wife. 'She said she had an itch. Even if this were true, she should be so sweetly numb with cold that such an irritation would pass unnoticed. But I do genuinely believe she was . . . she was rubbing her hands together for *warmth*.'

Tin Nose breathed out through a nose that was like a wolf's snout.

'Others are beginning to notice these things too,' continued his wife. 'There is gossip about the castle. I tell you she has broken faith with the Cold. This will end in thaw and death.'

'You go too fast!' cried Tin Nose. 'What of

my promise to the old Witch? I gave my word I would turn the girl into a fitting queen.'

'I say Haggoth was wrong to expect such a thing. After all, the girl is not even of royal blood.'

Tin Nose glanced about. 'Speak lower, lady. Nobody but us knows she is adopted and not born to the throne, not even the girl herself.'

'Then, Thurbolt, perhaps it is time they did. It is now clear to me she is unfit to rule and always has been. The warning signs were there to see. Remember how easily she cried? And you can never make an icicle out of salt water.'

Tin Nose turned to her abruptly. 'What will you have me do?'

'She must be removed.'

'But she is the Queen.'

'She has broken the law.'

'But who will replace her?'

Lady Sybia touched his shoulder. 'Why us, husband. Who is more loyal to the Cold than Lord Thurbolt and his wife? And the wolves respect you.'

Tin Nose gave a snort, unhappy at the idea. 'Then gossip will say we did away with the new Queen for our own purposes.'

Lady Sybia smiled, or rather her numbed blue

lips formed a smile, for there was not a spark of warmth in it.

'They will not be able to if they believe it to be the work of another.'

Tin Nose frowned. 'Who?'

'The boy. The one with the bear. He's a person of no consequence at the castle and has already displayed a violently hot temper. What a perfect gift he is to us.'

'And when shall it be done?'

'As soon as possible. Tonight, when the traitor is asleep in her nice *warm* bed.'

'Very well,' agreed Tin Nose slowly. 'You have convinced me, lady. I shall see it done.'

'You will not be sorry,' she murmured.

Just then, as she spoke, the breeze changed direction, carrying a strange new scent to the wolves, a mixture of boy, bear, and fish. Growls and snarls broke out along the line.

'Someone is coming,' said Lady Sybia urgently. 'We should not be seen acting suspiciously together. Go, husband.'

Tin Nose cracked his whip. The wolves obediently set off, low and sleek, the runners of his sleigh cutting the snow like knives. Lady Sybia wheeled her white elk around and dug in her heels. The elk half reared, then dashed straight for the snow-drift where Temmi lay.

Temmi thrust his face into Cush's fur, listening as the creature's hooves galloped ever nearer. Then there was a silence as it cleared both him and the drift in a single leap, landed, and continued on its way. Lady Sybia had not even seen him.

For a long time Temmi didn't dare move. He held Cush tightly, trying to take in what he had just heard. The worst part was knowing that this was entirely his fault, since he had forced Agna to understand about fire and warmth. And because of that knowledge she was about to be murdered.

'We can't let this happen, Cush,' he whispered. 'We just can't.'

Suddenly he jumped up and raced towards the castle, tripping and falling in his haste.

Above him circled Cush, who scanned the horizon for wolves. There *must* be wolves. Why else would the boy be in such a wild panic?

## Chapter Twelve

First Temmi ran to find the dwarfs. As usual they were warming themselves by the fire in their secret cave—and also as usual they were squabbling.

'I'm oldest and biggest,' Wormlugs was shouting, prodding his chest with a finger. 'I should know.' (They were arguing over which of two cockroaches had the longest legs.)

'Oldest and biggest doesn't always mean rightest,' countered Kobble innocently. He received a firm pinch for the remark.

'Oh . . . I stand corrected,' he muttered.

'Stop bickering and listen to me!' cried Temmi suddenly bursting in amongst them.

They turned to him in surprise.

'I have just overheard Tin Nose and Lady Sybia planning to kill the Queen,' said Temmi. 'They're going to do it tonight when she is asleep, and tomorrow they will rule the High Witchlands in her place.'

Wormlugs sniffed and shrugged. 'Nothing to do with the dwarfs,' he said dismissively. 'Big matters pass clean over the heads of little men.'

'But don't you see, this is all our doing. They have guessed Agna has betrayed the Cold, and it was us and our fire that did it. We must do something to help her. We can't just stand by and let this thing happen!'

The dwarfs swapped unsure looks without meeting Temmi's eye. But suddenly Kobble jumped up. 'I agree with Temmi,' he said bravely; and seeing Wormlugs angrily flexing his fingers, pinched himself before the bigger dwarf had the chance to.

Wormlugs was still far from convinced: so Temmi said, 'Do you think you can live safely with Tin Nose as your King? What if he remembers all those times you tormented his favourite wolf and decides to have you thrown to Frostbite? Think, Wormlugs, what other use can he have for dwarfs?'

'Hmm . . . ' Wormlugs thoughtfully chewed the end of his beard. 'Yes, I think the boy may have a point. But what can we do?'

'We must go to Agna when she is alone and warn her.'

'We can do it when she is in her chamber last thing tonight,' suggested Crumbtoot.

Temmi nodded. 'But we must be sure to get there before Tin Nose and his scheming wife.'

The night came quickly to the northern lands, but the moon took its time to rise. Freeing itself of the mountains, its beams struck the ice castle and it gleamed all at once and dramatically, like a milky opal.

Temmi and the dwarfs crept out of the nursery, Cush with them, making himself known with an occasional flutter of wings. The passageway stretched into the distance and before them a billion crystals glinted in the snow carpet.

The dwarfs were very nervous. 'We shall hang by our beards for this,' Mudsniff kept muttering.

'If we do they're sure to hang me first,' growled Wormlugs, 'because I'm the oldest and biggest.'

'No they won't,' said Flywick.

Temmi shook his head in despair. Even at a time like this they still managed to argue.

They moved through the castle without meeting another soul, until at last they came to the royal apartments. The dwarfs elbowed Temmi to the fore and he touched the door with his fingertips. Slowly it swung open.

Agna was sitting on the edge of her bed looking rather bored and lost in the velvety folds of an ermine cloak, which she had pulled up close about her. As the door opened she guiltily threw it off and jumped up. Seeing Temmi and Cush and her dear funny old dwarfs she smiled briefly in delight, but then, remembering she was now Queen, her hands went to her hips and her expression grew haughty.

'How dare you burst—'

'Majesty,' said Temmi calmly, 'there is no time. We have come to warn you of a plot to take your life.' And he quickly told her what he'd overheard from Tin Nose and his wife.

Agna sat very still as she listened, petting Cush who was curled up in her lap. Afterwards she smiled in disbelief.

'They wouldn't dare raise a hand against me,' she said. 'You are wrong.'

'They think you have broken faith with the Cold,' said Temmi, adding cautiously, 'And it's true—you have.'

Agna shrugged. 'I am Queen. Tin Nose made a promise to my mother, the Witch. He would never break his word, not to her.'

'But that's just it,' cried Temmi. 'The Witch isn't your mother—at least not your proper one. You are her *adopted* daughter, only she never told you. I heard Tin Nose say so.'

Briefly the flash of friendly faces and the echo of voices returned to Agna.

'No, I don't believe you,' she said, desperately fighting free of them. 'It's not possible, these are just lies.'

'At least give us the chance to prove it to you,' said Temmi.

'How?'

'If you agree to hide yourself, we will make your bed appear as if you were still in it, peacefully asleep. Then in the morning we'll come back and see if anything has happened.'

'Very well,' agreed Agna. 'But I don't expect to find it has.'

The dwarfs, working together, scooped up snow from the floor and arranged it into a heap upon the bed. Then Mudsniff carefully draped the ermine cloak over it. To anyone not in on the secret, there was no reason to believe it was not a sleeping person.

'And just where do you intend to hide me?' asked Agna as they led her away.

'In our secret place. But don't worry,' Temmi quickly assured her. 'We shall put out the fire as soon as we get there.'

'No . . . please don't,' murmured Agna. 'I have dreamt about fire ever since you first showed it to me and I ache to be warm again.'

'As your majesty demands,' said Wormlugs with a sly smile, 'so shall it be.'


They kept themselves warm through the dark night; Temmi frying his fish in the frying-pan and Agna tasting cooked food for the first time, eating greedily when she discovered how good it was. Then, in the early hours, they crept back to the royal apartments.

In the doorway to Agna's bedroom they stood gazing in silent horror. Through the ermine cloak and carefully arranged snow, into the ice bed itself, was thrust an ugly twisted icicle.

There could be no doubt in Agna's mind now.

Angrily she clenched up her hands. 'I will have Tin Nose and his wife arrested and chained for this!'

But as she spoke a distant voice arose. 'The traitor

Queen is dead! Long live their majesties Thurbolt and Sybia—and may the Cold be unending.'

'They have outflanked you,' said Crumbtoot slowly.

'We shall hang by our beards,' groaned Mudsniff.

'We're not caught yet,' said Temmi fiercely. 'But our only chance now is to escape the castle.'

'Quickly—inside and close the door,' cried Agna. 'We'll go by the secret passageway.'

## Chapter Thirteen

Confidently Agna strode across to the ice bed and, taking care not to look at the murderous icicle, touched the bed at one corner. Immediately it slid back, revealing a flight of steps carved into the solid ice floor.

Temmi peered down it. 'Is the passageway really secret?' he asked.

'If you don't mind, I'd rather admire it from the inside,' said Mudsniff worriedly. In the corridor they could hear angry voices approaching and the occasional bad-tempered snarl of a wolf.

'Come on,' said Agna. 'Hurry down all of you.' She followed last, closing the opening, not with a push, but with a touch as before.

At once the light grew grey and dull, coming as it did through dense rippled ice. The roof was low enough to reach up and touch, and Temmi held Cush who growled softly at the confined space, remembering the cage that first brought him to the castle.

By this secret means they briefly returned to the nursery to snatch their warmest boots and cloaks (Agna had to borrow hers) and then it was back into the passage.

'This way,' said Agna. She let the others go by and hung back a little, ready to enjoy their amazement when they rounded the next bend. And then they were there. Despite the urgency of the moment, Temmi stopped and gasped.

The passageway had only two walls and a floor, all of equal size, with the walls meeting overhead in a point. Together, walls, floor, and corners acted like a prism, causing the entering light to be dramatically split into vivid rainbow colours, one colour running into the next like splashes of wet paint; and the colours were lurid—almost living: blood red and velvety purple, honeyed yellow and summer blue. Temmi reached out a hand to touch them and found that he could; while his other senses were tricked into tasting and smelling them. Green was mint;

orange was spicy ginger (or sometimes nutmeg); yellow was as sweet as sugar. (Although for the dwarfs the same colours were cabbage, tobacco, and tripe—and for Cush were probably as different again!)

When Temmi next looked, the dwarfs were busy licking at the walls and had to be dragged away.

'Oh, let us stay—just a bit longer!' wailed Kobble, who was particularly fond of tripe.

'No,' said Temmi firmly. 'Not unless you want to end up as wolves' meat.'

With the help of Agna he managed to drive the dwarfs around the corner, where they found themselves starting down a long flight of narrow steps, the ice around them once more colourless and drab.

At the bottom of the steps the party came to an unexpected halt, the way ahead barred by icicles that hung from roof to floor. The icicles were as gnarled as tree roots and far too thick to be broken with bare hands alone—not that this stopped Wormlugs from trying, because biggest and oldest naturally meant strongest too.

'Ugh!' he exclaimed in shamed defeat.

Brushing him aside, Agna stepped up and began running her fingers down the icy pillars. At her touch each one made a different vibrant note. Her hands worked faster and faster until the whole passage was singing. Then the icicles lifted—all together, like a portcullis. Staring out through the gateway, Temmi saw dreary snowland, but to reach it they first had to cross a narrow bridge of ice that spanned the ravine.

'Don't look down,' called Agna, crossing so nimbly that she made it look ridiculously easy.

The dwarfs bullied Kobble into going next, and only when he had inched to safety were they happy to follow. Temmi came last after releasing Cush from his arms; and, as he crossed like a man on a tightrope, Cush hovered beside him giving him encouragement.

Once Temmi had jumped to safety, they all stood together in the shadow of the castle, grinning and looking so smug with themselves for having escaped it, that it took a dash of Mudsniff's gloom to bring them back to their senses.

'This won't do us the slightest bit of good,' he announced. 'The minute we try to make for the forest we shall stand out against the snow like ants on sugar.'

Temmi saw what he meant, but he couldn't think how it might be avoided. Then he noticed

Agna take something from her pocket. It looked like a tiny, clear icicle. She raised the narrowest, most pointed end to her lips and her cheeks filled out as if she were blowing a horn — not that any sound was made.

Three times she did this, leaving Temmi wondering why and annoyed at the loss of precious minutes. Then he heard something approach and, turning around, at last understood what Agna had done. She had called up the Queen's herd of reindeer; and now the animals stood in a semi-circle around them, their antlers forming a prickly wall and their sweet hay-scented breath coming in steamy gasps.

'Quickly, get amongst them,' cried Agna. 'They will get us to the forest unseen.'

The reindeer appeared to understand what they needed to do. They set off, walking slowly in a dense group towards the trees. They were not afraid of young bears, dwarfs, or children, yet neither did they trample or jostle them. And they were so large that no one had to stoop or bow their head. Reaching the forest eaves, the herd simply turned and walked away in a different direction, leaving Temmi and the others safely deposited there.

Straight away they ran deeper into the forest, until all sight of the castle was lost.

'What do we do now?' asked Flywick.

'We walk,' said Temmi who, as he went striding off, knew it was only a matter of time before Tin Nose came in pursuit—and the wolves too, of course. If only their tracks didn't show so clearly in the snow . . .

Temmi led the way through the forest, weaving in and out of the trees. The others followed him in a silent line, nobody feeling much like talking. It was all so dull and dreary, especially after the helter-skelter excitement of the earlier part of the day. And when the journey wasn't dull and dreary it was because of shadows and innocent sounds that gave them unpleasant jolts. Temmi knew he drove them hard, never letting them rest for more than ten minutes at a time, and then without food and only with snow melted in their mouths to drink. But he couldn't risk their staying so close to the castle.

By mid afternoon the early shadows of night were forming. The silent trees stood like cones of snow, dark about their bases, glinting starlight at their crowns. Too tired to drag her feet another step, Agna simply stopped, and her weary body folded to the ground.

'I can't go any further,' she gasped, unable even to raise her head to face them.

It was then, in the distance, they heard a wolf's full-throated cry. Mudsniff nervously chewed his beard and Kobble's bottom lip trembled.

'Come on,' said Temmi harshly, and crossing over he roughly dragged Agna to her feet.

They set off again now more frightened than tired: knowing that wolves run their best in darkness. They hadn't gone above a hundred steps more when the forest abruptly ended and before them stretched a frozen river, its far side thronged with snowy pines.

Temmi went to scramble down its bank, but Agna stopped him.

'No, we mustn't cross here,' she said. There was such authority in her voice that Temmi unquestioningly obeyed and climbed back up again.

Closely they followed the river, Agna stopping now and then to listen. Listen to what? wondered Temmi. *The ice?* He and the dwarfs were also listening. Listening to the wolves, whose baying sounded nearer by the minute.

'We have to cross the river soon,' he blurted out angrily. 'The moon is up. They will spot us emerging from the trees.'

'Not here,' replied Agna firmly, her head turned like a hunter to catch the smallest sound.

The dwarfs crowded together, trembling and frightened, on the verge of mutinying. Then Agna stopped. She stood absolutely still, her face pure concentration. 'This is the place,' she told them.

The dwarfs swarmed forward.

'No!' shrieked Agna. 'It's important to cross one at a time.'

Temmi stared at her unable to understand, and yet there was something about her certainty that persuaded him she was right.

'I'll go first,' said Wormlugs. 'It's proper for the biggest and oldest to lead the way.'

'Save your breath for your running,' said Temmi. He could hear the wolves fast closing in around them, calling out for the joy of the hunt. No doubt this added speed to Wormlugs's legs, and Temmi watched him scramble up the far bank.

Crumbtoot went next, swiftly followed by Mudsniff, Flywick, and Kobble. Before Agna could argue, Temmi shoved her after them. 'Hurry!' he whispered.

Agna streaked out across the ice, running sure-footedly until she was safely upon the other side.

As Temmi prepared to follow, he heard a

sound so close it sent him slithering down the bank, stones and snow spilling before him and his running feet slipping on the ribbed ice as soon as they made contact.

In the shadows of the trees on the opposite side, Agna and the dwarfs watched him with an increasing sense of unease, each silently willing him on. They saw him reach the river's mid-way point, whereupon a dark shape confidently launched itself off the high bank behind him, hitting the ice and, still crouched, slid a greater part of the distance until it was snapping at Temmi's heels.

'Frostbite!' growled Wormlugs; and he kicked at the snow until he found a suitable pebble. He briefly weighed it in his hand then hurled it with force, striking Frostbite on the shoulder. The wolf staggered and fell, howling with indignation and surprise.

Hands meanwhile reached down to haul Temmi to safety.

'Look!' shouted Wormlugs, pointing back over the way.

Onto the ice now poured shadowy men with spears.

Flywick shuddered. 'And there's Tin Nose himself.'

With sword drawn, Tin Nose led his men forward, eager wolves at their feet. But then something appeared to be wrong. In the middle of the river they came to an abrupt halt, looking around them fearfully. Too late some men and wolves turned to dash back to land—but an ugly crack in the ice ran faster and overtook them. With the crack came a harsh splitting sound and the slurp of unleashed water, as the river's solid surface broke up into a jigsaw of islands.

On each island a scattering of Tin Nose's people suddenly found themselves clinging for their lives. But the ice was unstable and only needed to tip a little to set wolf claws scrabbling or throw men off balance—and then with a scream they'd slide over the edge and the black water swallowed them.

Crouched and humiliated, Tin Nose was hopelessly adrift. He saw Temmi watching him and tried to stand before thinking better of it.

'Don't believe you are safe yet, boy!' he roared. 'Best you keep checking over your shoulder! Best you sleep with one eye open looking out for me!'

His threat was more chilling than the night.

'Come on,' said Temmi to his friends. 'We

101

waste good time here.' And as he turned he suddenly realized something.

Cush was missing. In fact Temmi was unable to recall the last time he had seen him.

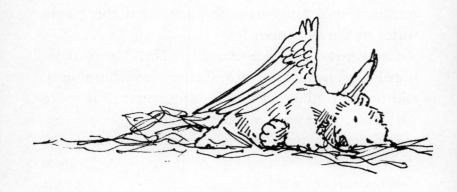

## Chapter Fourteen

Only after they had gone several more miles and were again deep into the forest, did Temmi dare risk their stopping and setting up camp for the night. The damp twigs took a while to get going into a blaze, yet once they had, there was enough fuel around to keep the fire burning brightly until morning. Of course they still had nothing to eat, so the dwarfs smoked their pipes, warming their fingers around the clay bowls.

Wormlugs remained in a bullish mood. 'Did you see how I hurled that boulder?' he boasted. 'And did you see Frostbite jump? I must be one of the best shots in the whole world . . . Why, I wouldn't be surprised if I didn't have the sharpest eyes too. You can't have one without the other . . . '

The dwarfs nodded sleepily. Wormlugs pinched Kobble because he did not nod as well as he might—but Kobble was already asleep.

Temmi sat a little apart from the group, glancing up from time to time at the branches. Agna knew who he was searching for. She crossed and sat on the log beside him, throwing her cloak around his shoulders.

'Cush is probably quite safe you know,' she said.

He glared up. '*Probably?*'

'Oh—I mean I'm certain that he is,' she added quickly. 'I expect he took fright when the wolves were closing in.'

Temmi nodded stiffly. He supposed she was right. Cush never did like the wolves, especially after Frostbite's savaging. Besides, thought Temmi, hadn't he always promised Cush his freedom and now he had it. But somehow he had believed the moment would be special—like the giving of a gift. He smiled bitterly. Could it be he expected something more, something like gratitude? Cush was only a bear after all and why should a bear understand such things?

'I hope Cush manages to find his way back to

his colony,' he said softly. 'It's a long way, even to fly.'

'Animals are cleverer than we think,' said Agna.

They were silent for a while, listening to the fire speak to them in crackles—as if telling them a story. Perhaps it was the one about the little flame who grew up to be a raging forest fire. Now and again the fire opened its mouth too wide and sparks flew out, fiercely bright among the stars.

Temmi gazed thoughtfully into the flames. 'Do you think we have seen the last of Tin Nose?' he asked.

Agna shrugged. 'At the moment I can't bring myself to think of anything but food. *Hot cooked* food. I'm *so* hungry.'

Hearing her words the dwarfs stirred restlessly.

'Food,' groaned Crumbtoot. 'What I wouldn't give for a few rashers of fried bacon—all sizzling and golden.'

'No,' said Flywick. 'A nice pork chop and the crackling just so.'

'Kidneys!' exclaimed Mudsniff. 'Slithering and chasing each other around the pan.'

Their squabble was suddenly interrupted by Kobble's loud snore. With a smirk Wormlugs dropped a twig into his mouth making him splutter.

'I think we all better get some sleep too,' said Temmi. 'We may feel better for it and tomorrow's journey is not going to be any easier.'

At the time Temmi had no way of knowing just how true his words would be. The journey certainly got no better, in fact it got a great deal worse. Leaving the shelter of the forest, they moved out onto the plains where the snow was heaped up and the wind never grew tired of its own bullying voice; and whenever anyone lifted their head to see an end to it, the whiteness simply ran on and on to the horizon, hurting their eyes.

They were cold at every moment of course, exhausted by it, even Agna who had lived most of her life in the cold. But they always felt better with hot food inside them.

In this, the rivers and lakes were as good as larders providing all the fish they could eat, once Temmi had managed to smash a hole through the ice and lower his line. At first he struggled because he had no bait, but with the help of some hairs from Flywick's beard he made a lure and then they simply waited.

Never has a fish been landed with such

excitement and applause as that one caught with the dwarf's surplus whiskers. After that it was much easier, as Temmi was able to use scraps of flesh to catch other fish.

'I think I shall soon turn into a fish myself if I eat another one,' grumbled Mudsniff several meals later.

'Why not?' said Crumbtoot. 'You already smell like one.'

But nobody really minded too much. They were so thankful to have food at all.

They trudged on, the second day sluggishly moving into the third day and dragging on into the fourth. Occasionally Temmi caught himself glancing up in the hope of catching sight of Cush, a hard habit to break; while at night he dreamed of Cush. In his dreams he was flying beside the bear, high above the trees. But in reality all that ever came from the sky were snow flurries.

On the fourth night they built camp on a narrow ledge of land, with a great sheltering mountain rising up on one side and a canyon on the other, dropping down onto jagged rocks at the bottom. In the sky over the mountains the northern lights shimmered like the hem of heaven.

Despite the cold, Temmi felt in good spirits,

with thoughts of his father and the village and how he might feel when he saw them again.

The fire burned cheerfully, and the fish he had caught the previous day spat in the heat of the flames. The dwarfs dozed, crushed up together like sparrows, their heads resting on each other's shoulders; and Agna stooped to pick up more sticks for the fire.

Then she dropped them with a loud gasp.

The dwarfs wriggled awake at once and Temmi spun around.

On the edge of the light, calmly watching, sat Frostbite and the wolf pack.

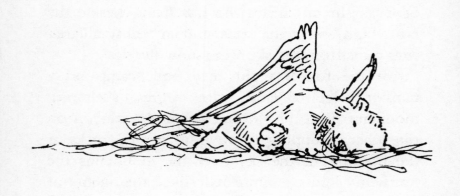

## Chapter Fifteen

Lacking weapons to protect themselves, the company followed Temmi's example by snatching burning sticks from the fire, which against wild animals are as effective as swords. However, Wormlugs was so busy running back and forth yelling 'Wolves! Wolves!' that Frostbite was able to take a daring chance. With a bound he came flying through the air, pinning the unfortunate dwarf to the ground; and roughly seizing him in his jaws began dragging him out of the light.

'Help! Help!' shouted the terrified Wormlugs.

It was horrible to hear him shout and squeal and not be able to do anything about it because the other wolves now pressed in, growling and pawing.

'I'm going to be eaten!' wailed Wormlugs.

'Hang on! Hang on, Wormlugs!' shouted Kobble, suddenly swishing round his brand into an arc of flaring light. A couple of young inexperienced male wolves jerked back and Kobble dashed through the space over to where Wormlugs lay clenched in Frostbite's jaws.

'Take that, you big bully!' yelled Kobble, stabbing the wolf with his brand. But Frostbite was loath to part with his prize—even now with his great bushy tail set alight. Flinging aside the brand, Kobble leapt at the wolf and because he was so small and light instantly became a rider upon the wolf's back.

This proved too much for Frostbite's dignity. Spitting out Wormlugs, he thrashed about in a frenzy—furious at the young dwarf and beside himself with terror at the fire which burned steadily and smokily and with the powerful smell of singeing. But no matter what he did, Kobble managed to stay in place, his voice jolted from him as he was bucked and twisted.

So grim was the struggle between dwarf and wolf, that the rest of the battle dwindled into a kind of half-hearted truce, while everyone (including the wolf pack) stood watching in disbelief.

Then Temmi realized a new danger faced Kobble and began to shout a warning. Agna joined in and all the dwarfs with her. They saw what blind rage prevented Frostbite from seeing. He was so anxious to be rid of both dwarf and flames that he had strayed dangerously close to the edge of the steep drop on to the rocks below.

'Jump clear, Kobble!' they all called. 'Jump while you still can!'

But as they watched, the wolf's claws lost the last of their grip. Desperately Frostbite tried to scramble back to safety, only to find it was too late. The ice was glass smooth and, sliding out of control, he and dwarf simply disappeared from sight into the dark, deep chasm . . .

The battle once more continued in earnest.

The wolves, far less concerned for the loss of their leader than the grief-stricken dwarfs were for Kobble, quickly gained the advantage. They rounded up the company like a flock of sheep and drove it away from the fire. Temmi, Agna, and the dwarfs drew closely together, their brands creating a wall of flames before them, but Temmi couldn't help worrying what would happen once the brands were burned out. The wolves bared their teeth and came crowding forward, snapping and growling.

Inch by inch the company was driven back to the rocks at the shadowy base of the mountain. Temmi wondered why and glanced over his shoulder. The darkness was as thick as fur. Then he saw something which sent a jolt through his body as sharp as any pain.

What he had caught at that moment was the winking glint of something small and gold from deep among the rocky crevices. It was the moon's reflection off a false nose. Tin Nose was lying in wait for them!

'Ambush!' yelped Temmi. 'Tin Nose is at our backs!'

Seeing no further reason to conceal himself, Tin Nose stepped into view, his grinning men coming behind with their spears. Tin Nose pointed his sword at Temmi.

'This time, boy, there is no easy escape. I shall personally see that you're hacked into broken meat for the wolves.' Then he turned to Agna. 'As for you, girl, you shall know how traitors are dealt with and will wish for such a *comfortable* death too, as you lie in the ice—frozen alive for a thousand years!'

He lifted his sword and beneath it the dwarfs quaked.

'First K-Kobble and now us,' sobbed Mudsniff.

But before the blade could fall, something large and white and powerful swooped from the sky like an angel, striking Tin Nose with the tip of its wing and landing with a swirl of snow.

Temmi unleashed his breath. 'Beog!' he gasped, recognizing Cush's father.

The mighty flying bear reared up on his hind legs, wings outstretched in an impressive display of size and strength. At the sound of his roar the wolves bristled: they knew the bear could break them with just a glancing blow of his paw. The men had their spears, but none dared risk wounding the creature, since a wounded bear is like a whirlwind with claws.

Tin Nose lay sprawled in the snow where he had fallen, glaring up at Beog with hatred. Seeing his face, Crumbtoot gave a squeak of horror, for his golden nose had broken free and without it his face was horribly like a skull.

'Is there not a man among you prepared to cut this creature down?' he shouted. When no one moved he leapt up brandishing his sword.

Beog growled a soft warning and, as Tin Nose lurched towards him, his claws slashed down, sweeping the sword from Tin Nose's hand as if no more harmful than a twig. Then he beat his wings hard, the down-draught nearly knocking the dwarfs off balance; and hovering about Tin Nose he caught his cloak in his jaws, then rose up with Tin Nose struggling beneath him like a monkey on a rope. Rising higher and higher, Tin Nose cursed everyone there and swore bitter oaths of revenge.

'You think this is the last of me,' he roared. 'But Lord Thurbolt is made of metal and ice, he does not flinch like soft warm flesh.'

He pulled out a dagger and slashed at his cloak. Instantly it ripped all the way across and Tin Nose dropped free of Beog, kicking at the air as he fell, and disappearing into the chasm without a sound.

As if this were a sign to attack, white bears came swooping down from every side, scattering the wolves and driving the men in all directions. The flying bears pursued them, diving low, their swan-like wings out-stretched and feathers ruffled; and the air trembling in their wake.

'We're saved!' cried Temmi throwing up his arms.

Feeling a playful nip on his neck, he spun around to meet Cush's face directly level with his own. The cub's entire body shook with pleasure and he immediately threw himself into Temmi's arms, licking his face all over and gently buffeting him with his wings.

Temmi found himself laughing and crying with happiness; and seeing Agna watching him with a puzzled look realized this was another warmth she had never known before. Love. In its place she had only experienced the coldness of duty.

The adult flying bears returned, some landing nearby, others wheeling above.

Wormlugs dabbed his eyes with his beard. 'Oh, if only Kobble were here to share this moment,' he sniffed. 'I would take his hand and shake it. Yes, I would warmly shake it and tell him that I, Wormlugs, may be the biggest and oldest dwarf, but he is certainly the bravest.'

Crumbtoot and Mudsniff solemnly nodded; Flywick removed his pointed hat and clutched it to his chest.

'Well, if you help me up, you can do these things for as long and as often as you like,' insisted a distant voice.

'It's Kobble's ghost!' hissed Mudsniff covering his eyes. 'It's come to haunt us for the times we were so unkind to him when he was alive.'

'Ghost be blowed!' replied the voice. 'Although I may soon turn into one if you leave me stuck on this ledge for much longer.'

They approached the cliff's icy edge with care. Lying on his stomach, Temmi spied Kobble on a spur of rock just under its lip and ordered the dwarfs to knot three cloaks together. This was done and lowered to Kobble. Then everyone lent a hand to fetch him back up to the top. When he appeared the dwarfs pounced on him as if they were wolves, not with teeth and claws but with hugs and handshakes.

'I never knew you thought so much of me,' beamed Kobble, his face flushed and happy.

Now they were all together again, Beog came lumbering forward, far less graceful on the land than he was in the air. He pushed against Temmi nearly knocking him over, although he did not mean to be so rough, and every time Temmi turned away Beog somehow managed to put his flank before him. At last Temmi understood. Gently he pulled himself onto Beog's back, sitting behind the ridge of muscle at the base of his wings.

Shyly other bears came up: one for each dwarf and one for Agna. They followed Temmi's example and minutes later were all sitting astride a flying bear.

Then Beog started to run: his paws pounded the ground and wings slowly fanned open. Temmi lay low along his back, gripping the bear's dense fur—and, happening to glance sideways, caught the tops of the trees sliding out of view.

## Chapter Sixteen

They rode with the wind blowing into their faces, gritty with snow. For Temmi and Agna and all of the dwarfs, the journey by flying bears remained breathlessly thrilling, each bear slightly rising and falling as his elegant wings rose and fell (so they could hear the great arching wing-bones creak like the branches of the trees when loaded down with snow). And not even the bitter cold could take the edge off their excitement. It only sent Temmi snuggling deeper into Beog's downy warmth.

Like migrating geese the bears formed a V-formation in the sky, with Beog at its head. Cush was the one blot on its neatness, flying close

alongside Temmi. Good-naturedly Beog tolerated him there; and Cush barked with joy, his wings flapping frantically to keep up, while his father's wings beat a steady stroke.

Without stars to navigate by and with all landmarks hidden in the deep well of night, Beog guided the bears by smell, his wet nose sniffing and twitching at the silvery-green-coloured wind.

And then at last Beog spread his wings and kept them rigid. Behind him the other bears did likewise. Now they no longer flew but glided, the air rushing hard over their feathers.

Temmi guessed this meant journey's end. He squinted up his eyes to see more and immediately they watered in the stiff breeze. Yet distantly he caught the glimmer of lights. Tears were blown from the corners of his eyes, which might have been a result of the cold, or again might have been simple tears of happiness.

Suddenly, and without a signal, the bears broke formation, spiralling downwards. The lake, forest, and huts of the village raced up to meet them. Yet when Beog touched down, it was done so softly, that the fluffy snow came up in a puff about his paws like wisps of smoke.

Sliding off his back, Temmi hugged the bear's neck. 'Thank you, Beog,' he whispered.

Not bothering to wait for the others, he ran stumblingly to the village. Cush attempted to fly after him, but Beog gave a low growl and Cush sadly turned back.

'Pa! Pa!' Temmi shouted as he reached the first hut.

Doors opened and heads cautiously peeped out. 'What's happening?' people asked.

'It's Temmi,' answered others emotionally. 'He's come back to us. Temmi's returned from the dead.'

Temmi's father's hut was one of the last to open its door. When the door finally did open, Temmi was shocked by the face that peered out at him—it was so drawn and thin.

'Is that really you, Temmi?' his father croaked, dry lipped. 'It will be too cruel if this is just another dream and I wake up by your empty bed again.'

Temmi proved he was no dream by flying into his father's arms and with such force that he nearly knocked him down.

All around them Temmi could hear the villagers rushing up or calling out his name. Then he heard a more hostile voice shout, 'Strangers! Strangers in the village!'

Remembering the others, Temmi pulled free of

his father's grasp. 'Agna and the dwarfs are my friends!' he protested. 'They mean no harm, Pa.'

'If they are your friends,' smiled his father stroking Temmi's hair, 'they are most welcome.' And he called: 'Show our visitors to the longhouse. We must hear all that Temmi has to tell us.'

Amidst growing excitement the villagers crowded into the long, low building. Agna and the dwarfs were already there; and, as most villagers had never seen a dwarf before (let alone five!), they attracted much comment. However, the villagers were very courteous towards them, if a little wary at first. The children were especially fascinated.

'Build up the fire,' ordered Temmi's father. 'Let's have light and warmth.'

Temmi glanced across at Agna and saw her readily nodding in agreement.

Temmi's story was a long time in the telling; and when he introduced Agna as a queen and the adopted daughter of a witch, the villagers gasped 'Ooh' and stared at her as simple people would. Queens were even rarer than dwarfs.

A startled cry, however, brought silence just as quickly and, turning from Agna, everyone stared at old Cuddie and Ebleen his wife, who held out her hand towards the girl, her fingers trembling.

'Agna . . . Don't you remember us?' asked the old woman in a voice barely above a whisper, but which carried to every corner of the longhouse. 'You were so young . . . a little child when you went missing in the forest.'

A buzz of excited whispers broke out all around Agna, who stood perfectly still in the middle of them, watching the fire with a hypnotized gaze. It was the biggest and brightest fire she had ever seen—so naturally the warmest too. Its blue leaping flames were so long that they broke in two, but all in the flicker of a moment; and around its edge little demon tongues lapped hungrily. Faces and voices swirled inside Agna's head—and a frozen corner of her memory finally melted.

'I remember the forest,' she said slowly, but as if to herself. 'The trees are green without any snow. Suddenly the Witch appears from behind a tree trunk and she stands watching me. She asks if I want to ride on the back of one of her wolves. I don't, but am too afraid to say. The Witch picks me up—her hands are so cold that I shiver—and she puts me on to her biggest wolf. Then it begins to run. It runs so fast that I can't get off. I call out for my mother and father, but we have arrived at the snowy mountains and I begin to get so very cold—'

'Look at us!' pleaded Cuddie. 'Don't you remember now, child? We are your true father and mother. You were stolen from us over forty years ago.'

Again excited whispers arose.

'But she is just a girl,' cried the blacksmith, bluntly speaking what most other people thought. 'How can what you say be true if it happened so long ago?'

Agna supplied the answer herself. 'In the Witch's domain,' she said, 'where it is always cold, even passing time can freeze. I know because Haggoth was over four hundred years old when she died.'

'And the Witch may have used her magic to fog Agna's memory,' added Temmi.

'A mother will always recognize her own child,' sobbed Ebleen, her hand still reaching out and trembling.

Agna felt all eyes upon her. In desperation she turned to Temmi. 'What shall I do?' she cried.

He smiled. 'Whatever the warmth inside you tells you.'

Agna didn't understand. She stepped hesitantly

up to the old couple, meaning no more than to drop a polite curtsy, but as she went by the fire she felt a curious glow inside that grew stronger by the second, quickening both her breath and footsteps—and then she was running; and reaching her new-found mother and father, she caught them in a great hug, sobbing uncontrollably until her face was red and blotchy.

Each dwarf discreetly wiped away a tear. Wormlugs claimed he had a speck of ash in his eye from the fire. Kobble, reaching across, gently pinched his cheek. 'Don't tell lies,' he said.

The events of the night were deemed worthy enough of celebrating and families brought out their precious jars of mead and cider.

'To Temmi, Agna, and the dwarfs!' was the toast. The dwarfs drank greedily, while the villagers stood by ready to top up their mugs with more. Alcohol had always been denied them at the Witch's castle since it refuses to freeze and warms the drinker's insides.

'Whidge iv p-erfloctly twoo,' hiccuped Wormlugs, his nose glowing red.

Much, much later, in fact closer to morning than midnight, the people returned to their huts. Amongst them were two reunited families.

Temmi and his father held each other as if one

was unable to walk without the aid of the other, which was rather awkward, not that they really noticed or cared.

Suddenly a great roar stopped them in their tracks, and looking up at the sky Temmi saw Beog effortlessly hovering there, and Cush bobbing along beside him. The cub wagged his stumpy tail and barked.

'Cush has *his* father back too,' cried Temmi in delight. 'But I'll still come and visit you, Cush. Every day. And I'm sure Agna and the dwarfs will want to come with me.'

Seeming to understand, Cush swooped down, licked the boy's face in mid-flight, and soared back up level with his father. Then, together, they slowly wheeled around and made for home.

# Other books by Stephen Elboz

## The House of Rats

ISBN 0 19 271664 6

Winner of the 1992 Smarties Young Judges Prize for the 9–11 age category.

*One damp foggy morning, the man who called himself the master threw down his napkin and strode out from the great house, never to return.*

Esther, Zachary, Carl and Frankie are happy, living in the mysterious great house, until suddenly the master vanishes and everything changes. The safe routines disappear. The wolves which roam the forest outside, howling for food, become a real threat; while inside the house, other people start to take over their lives.

Without realizing it, the children are in great danger. But then, just when they think there can be no escape, they meet one of the 'Rats'. And they begin to discover the secrets of the amazing house.


'I loved the vividly realised characters, the warmth and wit of *The House of Rats*. This is a fine novel.'

*Times Educational Supplement*

'A brilliant story which grips you from the first to last page.'

*Mail on Sunday*

## The Games-Board Map

ISBN 0 19 271701 4

*Beware of snakes, especially the slippery-backed varieties which are most treacherous of all.*

When Hebe begins the games-board adventure, it takes her a while to realize what is going on. But soon she has to believe that the impossible is happening all around her. From the musical chairs (who sing, of course), to bats and pirates, it's a crowded world. Hebe has to share the games board with all kinds of creatures: the bishop from the chess game who complains about 'those confounded draughts'; various pawns (or prawns?), and probably snakes too—after all, there are ladders.

What Hebe really wants to do is to get home, eventually. But it's not as easy as all that . . .

'A most unusual, original and inventive book.'
*Children's Books of the Year*

**Bottle Boy**
ISBN 0 19 271718 9

Treasure isn't always gold and silver, as Mouse discovers.
There's a fortune to be made from old glass bottles if only you
know where to look . . .

Mouse escapes from a life of crime and hardship, and sets off
to find his treasure. But instead he finds a whole lot of new
troubles. There's the Pendred Gang, who instantly become his
sworn enemy; the strange old man with a shotgun; the
everyday struggle just to survive. And it's not long before
Mouse's past catches up with him, secrets are revealed, and the
real danger begins.

'A superb thriller for nine- to 12-year-olds.'

*Sunday Telegraph*

'This is Stephen Elboz' third novel which will add to his
reputation as a stimulating writer for children.'

*Junior Bookshelf*

# The Byzantium Bazaar
ISBN 0 19 271578 X

'Bridie wondered what would happen if she wrote the truth.
  *Dear Aunt Dolly . . . Gramps disappeared into thin air . . . am
living with complete strangers in a condemned building . . . spend most
evenings with tramps. . .*'

Bridie's grandfather has vanished, and the menacing Crickbone
brothers have taken over his yard. Suddenly Bridie finds
herself all alone in the city. It never looked so strange and
threatening before. But then she begins to discover friends in
the unlikeliest of places, and ends up meeting Miss Firbanks,
owner of the Byzantium Bazaar, a department store where time
stands still and dust covers everything.

Now all Bridie has to do is solve the mystery of what
happened to Gramps, and for that she enlists the help of the
street people.

Don't expect Aunt Dolly to approve . . .


'Another thrilling story from the author of *The House of Rats*.
The scene is vividly painted and peopled with strong,
believable characters . . . an enthralling read.'

*Carousel*

'This is a wonderfully inventive madcap romp with a cast of
oddball but entirely sympathetic characters. It is reminiscent of
the best of Mervyn Peake.'

*The Times Educational Supplement*

## Ghostlands

ISBN 0 19 271740 5

*'Oh, this is a night to be out and haunting!' he cried. 'Come on, Ewan, come with me. We can go haunting together.'*

From the moment Ewan arrives at Doctor Malthus's house he realizes his is to be no ordinary visit. For a start there is Ziggy . . . who is a ghost. And where there is one ghost there are bound to be others.

Ewan quickly discovers that just because you are dead it doesn't mean you can't be in terrible danger, too. The local ghost-nappers are out to get Ziggy and are not above a spot of devious magic to help them. And just what has Ghostlands, the nearby theme park, to do with all this?

This is a ghost story with a difference — witty, sharp, and funny — in Stephen Elboz's inimitable style.

'Stephen Elboz is an exciting new literary talent who is rapidly establishing a reputation for unsettlingly supernatural stories . . . A shudder a page, scintillatingly written.'

*The Independent*